Oni
Rise of Shadow

C. L. Rue

Oni
Rise of Shadow

Olympia Publishers
London

www.olympiapublishers.com
OLYMPIA PAPERBACK EDITION

A CIP catalogue record for this title is
available from the British Library.

ISBN: 978-1-80074-028-0

This is a work of fiction.
Names, characters, places and incidents originate from the writer's
imagination. Any resemblance to actual persons, living or dead, is
purely coincidental.

First Published in 2021

Olympia Publishers
Tallis House
2 Tallis Street
London
EC4Y 0AB

Printed in Great Britain

About the Author

C.L. Rue was born in Milton Keynes but raised in Camberley. Working various jobs in the past, most recently as a receptionist, it was during his temporary job working night shifts that he decided to start creative writing. 'Oni — Rise of Shadow' is his first book.

Chapter 1

It was a cool, crisp night in Yoshino. The cherry blossoms were in bloom and the moon was lighting up the mountain. The only noise you could hear was the trees rustling in the wind. The silence was abruptly broken by the sound of footsteps. Three friends with backpacks and flashlights were walking through the trees, heading to the Mikumari Shrine.

"Can someone tell me why we are coming here in the middle of the night and not during the day, when we can see?" one girl asked. She was wearing a black, puffa jacket with a fur-lined hood. She had dark leggings on and was wearing knee-length boots; her dark clothes accenting her shimmering, gold hair.

"You ask this every time Triss and we give you the same answer: Jak doesn't do crowds, plus anything we find that is hidden is ours for keeps. Besides, think about it, would we be able to do this when there are tourists around? Staff doing tours? We are talking prison time, trying to lift something," responded a tall, athletic man. He had medium-length hair, just slightly poking out of his beanie, wearing dark jeans, black hoodie and black trainers.

"Zeke is right. These things are always rare and because

they are hidden, we can't get in trouble, at most we will get a small fine and a slap on the wrist for trespassing. As for crowds? I hate people. Anyway, quieten down; we don't know if they have security here and we are close to the shrine now," added Jak, the third of the trio. She was short, dressed in a hoodie with her hood up, her fiery, red hair falling out of her hood dropping down to her waist. She was also wearing black jeans and black trainers.

As they arrived, they scoped out the site. There was no security, just a couple of cameras that only looked into the entrance, which they were not going to use. They arrived at the back and climbed over the walls into the shrine. The three split up, to take different sections and cover more ground. It has a unique architecture compared to other shrines they had visited. This is what piqued their interest in it.

About half an hour had passed since they arrived and they had found nothing. They were about to give up and head back as they had some good photos of the site and didn't see much point in spending any more time there. However, Jak still had a feeling they were missing something. She went to where Triss looked, to see if she had missed anything (it wouldn't have been the first time). When Jax entered, she saw a small ken unit in the centre and felt drawn to it. "Hey Triss, did you check out this part?" Jak called out.

"Yes and no. I couldn't open the gates, its barred from the inside," Triss explained.

Jak continued to investigate the unit to find the entrance Triss mentioned. It was very unusual. Built over the doors were solid, wooden bars like a gate; it was like a mini fortress. She found the entrance and as Triss said, it was locked by a drop bar from the inside. All she needed was to lift the bar and the door could be opened. There was a small gap where she could poke something through but it had to be strong enough to lift the bar.

"Hey Zeke! Do you still have that rebar attached to your pack?" she asked, in hope.

"Of course! Never know when you are gonna need it!" he replied. Zeke was a bit of a hoarder. If he used something once, he would hold onto it for dear life in case he needed it again. The only reason he had the rebar was because he used it to pry open some floorboards in his college apartment for hidden storage. Jak never found out how he ended up with it in the first place.

He brought over the rebar to Jak who then managed to wedge it into the gap. She positioned it under the bar so as not to damage the gate frames, giving away that someone had been there. She started to try and lift the bar. It was really heavy and she only lifted it so far but she couldn't get it high enough to open the gate. "Zeke give me a hand with this." He came over and began to help lift the bar. It was a struggle as there wasn't much room for both of them to get a good grip, so they faced each other and overlapped their hands. Whilst holding the far end, they pushed down whilst pushing up on the part nearer to the gate. After a good couple of minutes of struggling, they managed to lift the bar high enough. Jak quickly pulled open the gate while Zeke used all his strength to keep the bar lifted.

As the gate opened, they saw a narrow, spiralling staircase leading deep underground, covered in dust and cobwebs.

"This looks promising," Jak exclaimed, the slightest hint of excitement in her voice. "Triss, Zeke, you guys stay up here and keep watch, I am going to go down and have a look." Zeke and Triss looked down the staircase, then at each other and agreed without hesitation. Jak pulled out a flashlight and proceeded to make her way down the staircase, making sure not to get caught up in any webs, as well as making sure none of the steps were missing. Judging by the thickness of the dust, it was a very old staircase and could have fallen into disrepair.

She finally reached the bottom, the air heavy from being underground. She looked around but there wasn't much there, just dirt and a couple of broken pots. Then she found the doorway. As she approached it, she started feeling something coming from behind that door. She noticed carvings in the woodwork; it was faded and in Japanese, so couldn't translate it. This only made Jak more curious. She started to push open the door. It was a struggle as the hinges seemed to have rusted causing a lot of friction. As soon as the door opened a putrid smell came out; Jak quickly pulled up her scarf to cover her face.

As she entered the room, she saw hanging from the ceiling, lots of holly charms and fish heads. That would explain this god-awful smell, she thought to herself but she continued forward. There was a chair in front of her and sitting in the chair was a skeleton of what Jake assumed to have been a Samurai, based on the armour it had on. "Guess I found out how the gate was locked from the inside, tough break," she mumbled to herself, slowly walking past him.

Within an instant she froze, as her eyes snapped onto something in the darkness. She couldn't explain how she knew something was there, it was just a feeling she had. She slowly raised the torch in her hand and in the distance, there was a wooden pedestal with a glass case on it. She continued cautiously. As she walked up to it, she was trying to make out what was in the case but it was too dusty to see into it. As she arrived, her heart beating out of her chest with nervous excitement, she wiped away the dirt and saw what was inside: a scroll and a small dagger.

The scroll had golden rollers and had been wrapped in a fine, purple, silk cloth whereas as the blade had a fine, black holster with a faded, golden pattern running around it. The handle was wrapped in a fine, black ribbon with purple detailing on the hilt. What was strange was the blade had been sealed in the holster by a wooden clip. This had carvings on it but the glass was too dirty to make out what it said. Jak wasn't that fussed about the blade; she was hypnotised by the scroll, thinking of the secrets it could contain.

She further inspected the box and realised it couldn't be opened; it was sealed shut and airtight. She took the back end of her flashlight and started to tap the glass, getting more and more forceful. She was trying to crack it instead of full-on smashing it, to reduce the risks of any damage to the scroll. Success. The glass cracked and she pushed in one of the bigger shards, then carefully pulled out the rest, creating a large enough gap to extract the scroll and the blade. She stashed them in her bag and began her journey to return to the others.

As she returned to the top of the staircase, she saw Zeke and Triss sitting next to each other looking rather cosy; Jak decided to sneak up on them. She crept closer and closer. "SURPRISE!" she yelled. Zeke startled and jumped up whereas Triss let out an ear-piercing scream.

"You are such an ass" Zeke chuckled, brushing himself off.

"Why do that to me?" Triss yelled, frustrated and embarrassed.

"It was funny! Anyway, let's go back to the car; you are

not gonna believe what I found."

The three friends returned to the car as Jak told them about the scroll and the sword, the body and the charms hanging from the ceiling; both Zeke and Triss hanging on to every word, thinking about how much they could get from this scroll.

The three journeyed back to Tokyo. It was a long drive but they preferred driving over flying. Triss was lying across the back seats asleep, her coat laying on top of her like a blanket as Jak and Zeke sat up front. Zeke was driving and Jak wasn't able to sleep; she couldn't stop thinking about the scroll.

"So, have you properly looked at the scroll?" Zeke asked. He turned down the stereo so they could have a proper conversation.

"No not yet," she responded. She opened her bag and retrieved the scroll. Jak removed the silk wrapping to find the scroll had been tied shut with a ribbon, attached was a note.

"Interesting…" Jak trailed off, lost in thought.

"What does it say?" Zeke enquired, his glance occasionally bouncing between the road and the scroll.

"I don't know, I can't read it, must be an old form of Japanese," Jak replied.

"Shit, neither can I," Zeke said, taking a peak at the label. "and Triss… well you know, is Triss. She wouldn't learn a new language even if her life depended on it."

"We all know someone who can though and he lives and works in Tokyo," Jak exclaimed. Zeke pondered for a minute, his mind blank about who she could possibly be talking about, then the penny dropped. "Toshi! Are you sure he will want to talk to us? You know he and Triss didn't exactly end on good terms when they split."

"It has been a year and besides, he wouldn't be mad at us.

If it comes to it, Triss can wait in the car," Jak responded.

Triss and Toshi used to be together. He was so in love with her, then about a year ago, Triss cheated on him leaving him heartbroken. He hasn't spoken to the group since. Jak hoped that enough time had passed that he has moved on.

They arrived in Tokyo at about 8 a.m. They went to the hotel room they were staying in, got washed and changed then headed to the Tokyo National Museum where Toshi worked. As they entered, they saw all the amazing artefacts and artwork on display, so perfectly preserved. They spent a good fifteen minutes wandering around until Jak located Toshi. He was a tall, slender man, dressed in a smart suit with short, black hair. Triss saw him and instantly pulled Jak and Zeke aside. "Why didn't you tell me we were seeing Toshi! Why are we seeing him anyway? He left us!" Triss said, using an angry hushed tone. Zeke shrugged and rubbed the back of his neck, trying to find an answer but couldn't.

Jak stepped in. "One. The reason we didn't tell you is because you would react like this. Two. We need him to read the note on the scroll, see what it says and if he knows what it is, he can tell us how much it could be worth. Three. The reason he left was because you slept with someone else, so suck it up princess." Jak was very upset with what happened between them; Toshi was like a brother to her. She personally doesn't have an issue with Triss but when she tries to make it about her, something inside her just snaps.

"Ugh fine, but note I am not happy about this," Triss groaned.

"Noted, now this way please, your highness," Zeke said mockingly.

Jak was in front, followed by Zeke with Triss trailing

behind, with a grumpy look on her face. Toshi had finished talking to a visitor when he spotted Jak and Zeke. "Jacqueline! Zeke! I can't believe it's you guys! How have you been?" He immediately gave Jak a massive hug then shook Zeke's hand.

Jak replied, "We are really good. Also, you know I don't like my full name! Call me Jak," she said with a laugh.

Then Toshi noticed Triss. "Oh, it's you, hi Triss," he said with discontent.

"Hi Toshi, how are you?" Triss said. you could feel the awkward tension.

"I'm fine thanks." There was a brief pause as no one knew what to say, then Toshi turned to Jak. "So am I to assume as you are all together and this is not a social visit?"

Jak's smile faded. "Unfortunately, there is an agenda," Jak explained. "On one of our 'trips', we found two very interesting items we need you to take a look at."

Toshi sighed. "Why am I not surprised?" He let out a small laugh. "Okay, well as these items are shall we say, 'not for the public', let's go to my office for some privacy."

As they arrived in the office, Toshi closed the door and closed the blinds on his windows. "Okay, what do you have for me and where was it located?" Toshi asked. Jak pulled out the scroll and the sword.

"I found these at the Mikumari Shrine in Yoshino. They were in a hidden room with a dead body and surrounded by the charms of holly leaves and fish heads."

"Did you take the sword from the body?" Toshi asked, trying to gauge how used it was.

"Nope, both the scroll and the blade were sealed in a glass case, it was very strange. The scroll has a note attached; maybe it can tell you what it is?"

"Okay, let's take a look." He unwrapped the silk round the scroll and started reading the note, his face unchanging as he read it. As he finished, he started muttering something so quietly no one understood. He got up and went to his bookshelf, scanning through many history books and grabbed one. He flicked through it, put it back and returned to his desk. Toshi rubbed his eyes in thought then finally spoke. "How familiar are you with Japanese history and legends?" The three all looked at each other, exchanging rather confused looks. Jak returned to face Toshi and before she could respond, Toshi began to explain.

"From those looks I guess not very. Well, back in 1604 Toyotomi Hideyori commissioned the shrine's main hall to be built, so I guess the 'secret room' was the real project. His father, Toyotomi Hideyoshi was the regent to the emperor of Japan until he passed away from a sickness." He took a pause to have a drink of water. Zeke stepped in.

"So this scroll belonged to one of the regents of the emperor? Sweet!" as Zeke was doing a little dance, thinking of the payday from this. Toshi interrupted him.

"No this did not belong to him, well it did, but not originally. Have you ever heard of Fuma Kotaro? Don't know why I asked, of course you haven't." He said it almost as an insult, though unintentionally. "Well, Fuma Kotaro was the leader of the Fuma ninja clan; he was the originator of the scroll, potentially." Triss stepped in.

"Potentially? Well, was he, or wasn't he?" Toshi just looked at her.

"I was getting to that before you interrupted. Please save all questions till the end." Triss just rolled her eyes and folded her arms.

"Where was I, oh yes Fuma. So, the legend is that Kotaro was part Oni, a demon. He was considered the rival of Hattori Hanzo, a legendary warrior of his time. Well, a favourite story is that Hattori Hanzo was killed by Fuma Kotaro in 1596. However, there is one story that is the most interesting. It goes that whenever the two fought each other, they would be so evenly matched that they couldn't kill each other, so Kotaro decided there was only one way to beat Hanzo; he summoned a full-blooded Oni. This would be the first and only time he used his Oni blood to do something this dangerous and unpredictable. So, he summoned the creature and used it to kill Hanzo." Jak was about to ask if it was the scroll that summoned the creature but then thought she should wait until he had finished. "Anyway, as it goes, the Oni after killing Hanzo, grew very powerful and Fuma realised it was too dangerous to be kept around; so he sealed it within a scroll. Fearing it would be lost in the wrong hands, he sent it to Hideyoshi to guard the scroll until he could come up with a way to defeat the Oni. As he got ill, he passed the scroll to his son, who had it locked up in an undisclosed location."

Zeke, Jak and Triss stood there in awe of the story Toshi told, eyes drawn to the scroll, mouths agape. There was silence for about a minute, then Toshi chimed in. "That's if you believe the stories, it's most likely just a diary page or something like that. Onis and dark magic aren't real, so let's read it shall we? Jak will you do the honours of breaking the seal?" Jak finally snapped back into reality, looking at the scroll. She was concerned about reading the enclosed. She had never been the superstitious type but something about this felt wrong, like there was something telling her not to break the seal. Yet, at the same time, there was something about the scroll that enticed her, almost making her want to open it; this inner conflict was fighting throughout her entire being. She picked up the scroll, the voice telling her to open it was getting stronger. As she was preparing to open the scroll, one of the employees entered. She quickly stashed the scroll in her bag before they could see it.

"Ahh Kukiro, how can I help?" Toshi asked, getting up from his chair and heading to the door, trying to obstruct her view as he approached her.

"I was wondering if you were ready for lunch. If you are busy, I can come back later."

"No, no I will come with you, just give me one minute okay?" Toshi responded. The two quickly exchanged a kiss, both Zeke's and Jak's mouths dropped while smiling at the same time. Triss, she did not seem pleased. Toshi turned around to face them. "So, shall we continue this after I finish? Say ten o'clock at mine?" Zeke was the first to bring it up.

"Toshi you stud! Who is the fox?" he asked, clearly happy for his friend.

"We started seeing each other around two months ago, it's not a big deal seriously, so yes tonight? I'll cook!"

They agreed to meet Toshi at his place at 10 p.m. and the friends parted ways, looking forward to tonight. Jak however, still had this feeling that it was a bad idea but she kept reminding herself, what harm could it do?

Chapter 2

Jak was the first to arrive at Toshi's. He lived in a stunning three-bedroom apartment, which had a great view. Jak was in awe of how well he was doing for himself. Toshi was never really good with his money when they all used to hang out, or so she thought but then again, he would usually spend his money on Triss.

"Can I offer you something to drink? Beer? Wine? Or a soft drink perhaps?" Toshi asked. He was such a nice person, Jak missed him after he departed from the group.

"A glass of water will be fine for now, so what happened after you left, Tosh? What did you get up to?" Toshi was in the kitchen getting a glass of water. As he emerged, he responded.

"Not much really. I was a mess after what happened between me and Triss; I was miserable a lot of the time. I continued travelling for a bit checking out landmarks but it was never the same without you guys. I eventually got bored of it and decided to settle down. Luckily, I had saved money from our last expedition as well as money made on travels; I managed to get this place and eventually got a job at the museum."

"How come you never tried to call? I've missed you so

much," Jak asked, a hint of upset in her voice.

"I'm sorry, it just didn't feel right at the time. I know now that I should have but I wanted to focus on myself and getting settled in first. The more I put it off, the more I just ended up finding reasons not to call. Besides, even if I tried you aren't exactly the easiest person to contact. How often do you guys move around?" Jak could see that Toshi meant it as his eyes dropped down and looked like he was about to cry. She reached over and took his hand, giving him a warm smile as he looked up.

"It's in the past. What matters is that you are doing well for yourself and you've moved on, it seems," she said cheekily. "So, tell me about Kukiro!" she added.

"Not much to tell really, she is a very quiet person, doesn't really tell me much about her life before the museum; all I know is that she is an orphan." Toshi sounded sort of disappointed, in truth he was. He thought that since they had been dating for a couple of months that she would be more open about her past but any time he brings it up, she shuts down and avoids answering anything.

"Ahhh, a woman of mystery," Jak added. She could see that Toshi was becoming uncomfortable talking about this so decided not to pry any further and left it at that. They spent the next hour reminiscing about their past escapades, both with the group and before then. Toshi and Jak have been friends since they were kids. They always used to pretend they were adventuring across mountain ranges, hiking through the Amazon; they always wanted to travel and see the world. Toshi and his family moved to the States when he was just a baby. After Toshi finished high school, his family moved back to Japan but Toshi opted to stay and finish college with Jak. That was where they both met Triss and Zeke. After college, they all went travelling and just never stopped after that. They sat there laughing and having a great time when suddenly there was a knock at the door. They realised they had been sitting there for over an hour; Toshi hadn't even started cooking. Toshi dashed into the kitchen to start cooking their food, Jak went to answer the door and to her surprise, it was Kukiro at the door. Kukiro looked quite surprised herself seeing Jak open the door. "Oh, I wasn't expecting you to be here, is Toshi here?" Kukiro said, a hint of concern in her voice, understandable considering the situation.

"Yes, he is, Toshi! It's for you!" she called out to the kitchen. "I am Jak, we didn't get a chance to introduce ourselves before, I am a friend of Toshi's."

"Oh, you're the famous Jak! Toshi speaks so highly of you, I'm Kukiro, it's a pleasure to make your acquaintance," she said, a sigh of relief was released after hearing that name. Toshi speaks of Jak like a sister and Kukiro was genuinely excited to meet her.

Toshi came out of the kitchen. "Kukiro? What are you doing here? Is everything okay?" he asked, concerned. Kukiro was never one to drop in out of the blue.

"Yes, I am fine. I just wanted to see you and thought I would surprise you. I didn't realise you had friends coming over, I can go." Jak immediately stepped in.

"Please don't go, join us! There will be plenty of room and I would love to get to know the woman who has captured Toshi's heart!" she exclaimed, giving Kukiro a wink, with a huge smile on her face. It was a gift Jak had. Everything she did was so warm and inviting, even if she wasn't the most social person; it made Toshi happy to see that Jak was making an effort.

"Yes, please join us, I insist," Toshi added, extending his hand to Kukiro. Hesitant at first, she took Toshi's hand who pulled her in for a kiss and hug. Kukiro blushed, slightly embarrassed but at the same time she loved it. Just as Jak was about to close the door, Zeke came crashing through.

"Whoa! Were you about to close the door on us, how rude!" Zeke said mockingly. Triss trailed in behind, her blonde hair flowing. She's really made an effort Jak thought, she was wearing one of her best dresses and had done her makeup as if she was going on a date; she didn't want to win Toshi back did she? She obviously did but Triss fell into a foul mood seeing Kukiro.

"Why is she here?" Triss said abruptly She wasn't the best with other people but this was something else. It was an ugly side of her you would rarely ever see; jealousy. Kukiro instantly withdrew, she felt really awkward now, as if she was imposing on the evening.

"She is joining us; this is my home and she will be staying. Do you have a problem with that Triss?" Toshi responded in a rather authoritative manner, laying down the law. He was not about to have his girlfriend take this undeserving abuse.

Triss just huffed and sat down, frustrated she put in all this effort and now couldn't do anything.

"Maybe I should go," Kukiro whispered to Toshi. Toshi instantly turned to her and held her hands.

"I won't hear of it; you are staying!" Toshi insisted. He took her coat and hung it up by the front door. The group all sat down, making conversation while Kukiro and Toshi headed to the kitchen.

"Triss, you need to chill out," Jak said in a hushed tone,

so as not to be heard from the kitchen. "I know what you are trying to do and you need to knock it off now. Toshi has moved on and is with Kukiro now." Triss looked taken aback or about as fake as she could make it.

"Whatever do you mean Jak? I just wanted to look nice, if people notice then that's their business. Can't a girl make an effort? You should try it sometime," she retorted, trying to get under Jak's skin. Zeke could see Jak was getting more and more frustrated.

"Ladies please, try and be civil, we are guests. Jak you need to calm down, Triss don't be a bitch towards Kukiro. Please, I want us all to have a good time," Zeke said. Jak agreed, Triss was slightly offended being called a bitch but she couldn't disagree with the statement. She isn't sure why she was acting this way; she didn't feel anything towards Toshi. So she also agreed, even though it was half-hearted.

Jak, Triss and Zeke made small talk whilst Kukiro and Toshi were in the kitchen. "So, who is the girl who doesn't like me?" Kukiro asked, passing Toshi chicken she had just cut up into essentially, mini fillets.

"Triss? She is an old girlfriend; I told you about her, didn't I?" he said. Kukiro was taken aback.

"That's Triss? Why is she here? After what she did to you!" She took a moment to calm herself down.

"Kukiro, it's fine, I am over it, besides…" he paused and took her by the hips, "… I am with you now and I couldn't be happier." He then kissed her passionately. She let herself fall into the moment, as if there was nothing else going on in the world and no other person; it was just those two in that moment of pure ecstasy. She eventually snapped back to reality.

"Stop Toshi, we have guests to feed!" They managed to finish cooking and sat down with the rest of the group. They ate and drank and everyone seemed to get on, apart from Triss who made no effort with Kukiro, although no one was surprised really.

After they had eaten, Toshi and Kukiro returned to do the dishes, leaving the others in the lounge. "So guys, do you think this scroll could be the one Toshi mentioned? The one that could summon the demon?" Zeke asked, with genuine curiosity in his voice. Triss just scoffed at the notion of it.

"No way, magic and demons? Come on Zeke even you can't be that gullible!" Zeke just dismissed her.

"What do you think Jak?" he looked hopeful that he would get some support. However, Jak was still just as conflicted as she was since they were in Toshi's office. Most of her believes that it's just a tale and nothing more but there is a part of her, the part that feels drawn to it, that feels something every time she looks at and touches the scroll. She realised that she hadn't answered.

"I don't know to be honest. I mostly want to say that it's just a story and what we are holding is a normal scroll but some part of me believes it could be the real deal." Zeke looked sort of confused but then agreed with what Jak said. Normality dictates it is just a normal scroll but something about this one gave him an inkling that it could be real. Triss chimed in.

"Speaking of the scroll, how are we supposed to open it with her here?" Jak didn't rise to the jabs at Kukiro.

"I'm sure she will be cool. We will talk to them before we bring it out."

Before they could even bring it up, Kukiro and Toshi had come out from the kitchen. "Thank you everyone for a lovely evening, but I must be going, I'm helping open-up tomorrow, so need to get some rest." They all said their goodbyes to Kukiro who grabbed her coat and headed home. The group then gathered round the table to do what they planned; read the scroll.

Jak broke it out and placed it on the table. Jak looked worried. The feeling that what they are doing was a bad idea kept getting stronger. Toshi noticed and put his hand on her knee. "Jak, are you sure you want to do this? It will be just as valuable sealed and not knowing what's inside-" He was cut off.

"I am sure," Jak responded confidently. "My curiosity is too much to just ignore; I have to know what we've found."

Jak removed the ribbon tied around the scroll and unravelled it. The writing was in black but it shimmered, like a ripple of light was being shone across it. It was almost like it was pulsating. "Must just be a trick of the lights," Toshi said, sceptically. Even he wasn't sure why it was doing that. Everyone looked really unnerved by it. Leaving the scroll on the table, Toshi rotated it to face him so he could read it. "What does it say?" Zeke asked, almost trembling with anticipation.

"Give me a minute," Toshi replied, still scanning the scroll. His eyes darted through reading the passages. As he started to read, Jak noticed he was looking more and more terrified with each passing second. Jak's heart was pounding almost out of her chest. As he finished, Toshi turned to Jak instantly. "Quick, re seal this scroll n-" Before he could finish, the lights started to flicker in his apartment and a strong wind forced his windows open forcing everyone to shelter themselves. Suddenly, a dark smoke, heavy and thick was oozing out of the scroll and a bright light shot out of it. The four covered their eyes to shield them from the intense burning light coming out. All of a sudden, a shadowy figure appeared out of the light, then in an instant it disappeared. The light, the smoke, the wind and the figure all disappeared as if it hadn't happened. As the group collected themselves, they realised that the scroll was gone as well.

"Toshi, what did we just do!" Zeke yelled, still trying to process what had just happened. Toshi, with a look of disbelief in his eyes, was barely able to summon words. He finally managed to utter,

"We have released evil."

"What do you mean evil! It was just a story! These things don't exist! None of what we saw should happen!" Zeke yelled, picking Toshi up off the ground by the collar of his shirt.

"Zeke! Put him down now!" Triss screamed, tugging at Zeke's arm begging him to stop. Zeke eventually let go and Toshi collapsed to the ground. He was still shaken by what he had seen and couldn't find the strength to stand. As he sat there, he looked to his left and saw that Jak was unconscious. He found what strength he could to pull himself over to her.

"Jak? Jak! Wake up!" Toshi yelled, panicking. Hoping she was okay, he jostled her shoulders trying to shake her awake but it wasn't working. He then checked for a pulse and to see if she was breathing. Thankfully she was. Why won't she come to? he thought. She didn't get knocked by anything and she isn't one to pass out from fear.

Suddenly Jak shot up, sitting upright, her eyes opened wide as if waking from a nightmare. "What happened Jak?" Toshi asked. Jak got to her feet and started walking around, as if not hearing Toshi. "Jak?" he asked once more.

"I don't know, I just collapsed. Some feeling just took over me and before I knew it, everything was getting darker and then I woke up. What happened?" They all looked to Toshi, who looked at all of them; a fear of dread came over him as he remembered what he saw.

"I don't know how to explain it…" he said, a lump in his throat as he was so unnerved. "Someone, or something, came out of that scroll. I guess whatever it was, it took the scroll." Suddenly, the last words he'd read on the scroll flashed through his mind: '*Should you read this scroll you have already sealed your fate*'. He was struggling to remember the full passage he'd read.

"So, the stories are real? That means that what came out of it was an actual demon!" Zeke asked, full on freaking out, pacing back and forth frantically clutching his skull, as if being driven insane by thinking about what he saw.

"I guess so. So what do we do now?" Toshi asked, hoping someone would have an idea on how to handle the situation. He turned to Jak who was looking so confused, she seemed still dazed about collapsing; that and trying to process everything they witnessed. "Jak, what shall we do?" Toshi asked, hopeful that she would have an answer. "We need to find out where it went or where it will go." Triss, who had been abnormally quiet apart from sobbing faintly, noticed something on the wall. She looked at it but she couldn't read it. It was written in Japanese, burnt into the wall.

"T-Toshi? What does that say?" she stuttered, trying to compose herself, wiping away her tears. Toshi looked at the scorched writing and the fear in his eyes and face grew.

"It says…" He had to swallow the courage to say the next bit. "It says, 'I'm coming for you'." All of the friends looked

26

at each other, scared and nervous about what lay ahead for them.

All of a sudden, a crash came from the window. Broken glass surrounded a shadowy figure on their knees. They were masked and dressed in all-black garb. Zeke, out of instinct, charged the figure thinking if he can take it down now, they can forget this ever happened. The figure immediately sidestepped Zeke. It put their hand around Zeke's neck and turned him to face everyone else, then dropped Zeke to his knees and drew a blade to his throat. Jak, Triss and Toshi all stood very still, not taking their eyes off the stranger. They didn't want to anger whoever it was and cause any harm to Zeke.

The stranger looked at the wall and saw the sign. She immediately turned to the others. "Return the scroll and your friend shall be unharmed." Toshi instantly recognised that voice.

"Ku-Kukiro? Is that you?" The group all turned towards the stranger. Her eyes darting quickly between all of them, she realised her cover was blown and released Zeke. She dropped her face cover to reveal she was in fact Kukiro and Toshi was right.

"What the hell Kukiro! What are you doing!" Zeke said angrily, getting to his feet. "Well? Explain right now!" Zeke was clearly not happy.

"Please, there is no time, give me the scroll now and I can explain after." Jak pulled Zeke back as she could see his temper rising.

"We don't have it; whatever came out of it took the scroll." Kukiro looked really worried and frustrated.

"Then he has the scroll, I must go after him." She went for

the window.

"Umm, Kukiro?" Toshi said, very nervous about seeing this side of someone he thought he knew. "You can use the door, it's much safer." Kukiro turned round and saw the devastation in his eyes. She shook her head and ran out the door, feeling upset she may have lost the one connection she had. Jak instantly grabbed her bag and pursued after her.

"Kukiro wait!" she yelled down the street. She was so fast it was lucky Kukiro heard her and slowed down.

"I want to help you," Jak said, trying to catch her breath at the same time.

"You can't. No one can, it's my task and mine alone. I need to get that scroll back to imprison him again." Kukiro kept her eyes facing forward. She was so focused and confident in her stride, very different from the quiet girl she met that evening.

"I felt the energy from that scroll, you can't do this alone, let me help you." Kukiro stopped and grabbed Jak by the shoulder.

"Look Jak I appreciate the offer but please, return back to the others. The best way for you to help is to go back and look after each other at Toshi's apartment. Once I have done what I need, I will return and explain everything to everyone." Kukiro looked dead serious.

"Well, you can tell us all when we head back together!" a familiar voice shouted from across the way.

Zeke, Toshi and even Triss were following behind them. "Regardless of what happened up there Kukiro, you are still with Tosh and that makes you family. And we do not leave our family behind," Zeke exclaimed and Toshi and Triss nodded in agreement. Triss walked up to Kukiro.

"I know I was giving you a hard time earlier and for that I am sorry; you don't deserve that kind of treatment. And I am not just saying it because I know you could kick my ass in three seconds flat," she said with a chuckle; but she genuinely meant it. Zeke and Jak were impressed that Triss admitted what she was doing and that she had even apologised as well. Toshi was quiet but gave her a reassuring smile. He was still processing everything and trying to wrap his head around it. Kukiro looked round the group. She hadn't had this kind of support in a very long time; she truly felt gifted.

"Okay but stay close and if I tell you to run, you run okay? He isn't going to give anyone a chance." Again, she was very serious. They all looked at each other, worried that what they were doing was a mistake and they should have stayed at Toshi's but they knew it was the right thing to do. No one should have to face this terror alone, plus seeing Kukiro's resolve and composure in the face of adversity gave them the confidence they needed to see this through. They agreed and followed Kukiro down the street.

As they were walking down the empty roads, Triss pulled Toshi back. "Toshi, I want to say I am sorry. I shouldn't have acted the way I did." Toshi, more focused on the Kukiro, responded.

"It's fine Triss." She stopped him to grab his attention.

"It isn't, I think it is because deep down I still have feelings for you but I know our time has passed, we both have moved on from our past. I guess seeing you brought all these emotions back." Toshi just put his hand on her shoulder.

"You don't have to explain, it's fine. I forgive you and I am sure Kukiro does too. Let's just forget this happened okay?" Triss still felt bad but smiled at the thought of being forgiven.

Ten minutes had passed when they noticed scorch marks on the walls and they also seemed to have been clawed on. However, the group still pressed forward lead by the unfaltering Kukiro. When they turned the corner, they saw a clothing shop had been smashed in and the scorch marks lead to inside the shop. The group approached tentatively, nervous. "He is still in there," Kukiro whispered, so as not to alert the creature to their presence. "We need to split up, Zeke and Triss, you go up the left side, Jak and Toshi, up the right, I'll take the centre. Search around and meet back here, don't try to attack him if you see it and don't alert him to your location. If you see him, just back away slowly then come and find me."

Zeke answered in a hushed voice, "Are you sure splitting up is a good idea? That usually never ends well."

"It's the quickest way to cover more ground and at least you guys won't be alone; you all have each other," Kukiro replied, confident in her plan.

Jak, who was also worried, said, "Then why are you by yourself? Surely it would make sense if you were to join one of the pairs?" She brought up a good point but Kukiro just pulled out her sword and said with a confident smile,

"Who said I was alone?" they all split up in the agreed groupings and started to search the shop. They looked for signs of the creature and couldn't see any. It was quite dark so it was hard to see anything. Jak resisted the urge to pull out her flashlight; it would help her see but could also attract unwanted attention from the creature.

Zeke and Triss anxiously progressed through their section of the store. "So, what were you talking to Toshi about?" Zeke whispered.

"I was apologising," she responded, looking around for any signs of whatever came out of the scroll.

"Wow two apologies in one evening, aren't you maturing?" he joked in a hushed tone, stifling his laughter. Triss just smacked him on the arm.

"Focus! You heard Kukiro, this thing is dangerous!" she whispered.

As Toshi and Jak continued through the store, they came across a mannequin that had been knocked onto the floor and stripped of its clothes. They could just about make out darker marks on the doll, similar to those leading into the shop. They didn't know what to make of it until a shadowy figure grabbed Jak and darted out of the store, leaving a smoky trail.

"JAK!" Toshi yelled. "Guys! The demon grabbed Jak!" Everyone rushed to outside the front of the store where they got a proper look at the creature floating in the air, holding Jak by the throat. It looked like a man but he was as dark as the shadows. He was wearing a black, hooded, leather trench coat all buttoned up. He also had a mask on, covering his entire face. Through the darkness of the mask were two bright, white, piercing eyes.

"Drop her right now," Kukiro yelled, drawing her sword, posing ready to attack. The creature ignored her and focused on Jak. He looked her up and down, leaned in and breathed in her scent; he did a little shudder. With a deep, raspy voice he spoke. "You are pure of heart. I wonder how long it would take to break you." Jak fell unconscious.

"I said drop her now! I will not ask again Oni!" Kukiro yelled again, holding her pose not even flinching. The creature turned to Kukiro, this time dropping Jak.

"Foolish mortal, you dare challenge me? Do you know

31

who I am? I AM KAGE NO AKUMA, THE DEMON OF SHADOW!" The ground began to shake, his eyes burning brighter. Kukiro remained unfaltering in her stance.

"You don't have to do this the hard way. Just return the scroll and I will send you back to rest," Kukiro demanded. The demon reached into his coat and pulled out the scroll. He looked at it for a while, then without so much as a movement, the scroll ignited in his hand, turning to ash. He then floated down onto the ground and approached Kukiro with a swagger of confidence. Everyone was paralysed with fear. Jak still remained unconscious in a crumpled heap on the floor and Toshi was looking for an opportunity to reach her to see if she was okay. As soon as he tried to make a move, the demon looked at him, his eyes glinted and Toshi froze; he was stuck in place and couldn't move.

Continuing his approach to Kukiro who still hadn't made a move, he reach out and grabbed her sword by the blade with such swiftness that if you'd have blinked you would have missed it. He then moved the blade into his heart, until the two were so close they were breathing on each other. "I like the hard way," he whispered into her ear. He then pushed Kukiro back with such a force she was sent flying into Zeke, who managed to catch her but the force knocked him off his feet.

"Do you really think a normal blade would be able to stop me?" Kukiro struggled to get up to her feet. Akuma noticed the emblem on her chest.

"Is this the best the fallen lotus clan has to offer? Pathetic. Perhaps I should go to visit your masters to find a real challenge." He removed the blade from his chest and then snapped it like a toothpick. He floated up into the sky.

"Is that the best you got?" Kukiro uttered. She had just got to her feet but was still struggling to stand. The demon turned back, still in the air.

"You are persistent child but you are not worth my time. None of you are." As he turned to fly off, again he looked down at Jak; she was still unconscious. Then in the darkness came a voice in her head, "I'll be back for you."

Chapter 3

The group had made it back to Toshi's. Zeke carried Jak in, Toshi and Triss helped Kukiro. "Zeke put Jak on my bed, Triss help me lay Kukiro on the couch." Toshi delegated, trying to get a handle on what he just saw.

"I don't need to sit down," Kukiro announced. As she tried to move, she winced in pain and clutched her chest where Akuma pushed her.

"No, you need to, let us help." They laid her down on the couch and Triss went to get ice.

"Please I have to go to get him. Let me go." Kukiro tried to explain but she didn't have the strength to stand, let alone travel.

"You are in no condition at the moment; besides, you saw what he did! He took you down without so much as making a fist!" Toshi yelled, trying to talk some sense into her.

Triss returned to the couple, with ice wrapped in a towel. Toshi took it and placed it on Kukiro's chest; she winced again. "Before we go anywhere, we need you to recover." Kukiro tried to sit up to oppose but it was too much effort in the state she was in. She just collapsed back onto the sofa and accepted the inevitability that she would need time to recover. Zeke came back into the room. "Jak is still out cold but she is breathing. How is Kukiro?" Zeke asked.

"I think she might have some bruised ribs, possibly cracked but some rest and she will be fine. What about you? You did have a woman launch into you and you landed flat on your back," Toshi asked, concerned for his friend.

"I'm fine Tosh, strong as an Ox!" he said beginning to flex. Toshi and Triss were amazed he could be so light-hearted. Triss instantly went in.

"This isn't a joke Zeke! Our friends are hurt and you are making stupid comments! What is wrong with you!" She was trying to hold back her tears. Zeke put his arms down and his smile faded.

"Because humour is how I process things; if I didn't, I would crumble! After seeing what we just saw? It is literally driving me insane that all of this is real and I can't do anything to stop it!" This was the first time Zeke had seemed really serious. Triss backed off as she could see the pain in his eyes. Toshi tried to break the tension.

"Look, everyone is frazzled. I think we all need to get some sleep. Triss why don't you go and sleep with Jak and just keep an eye on her, make sure she is okay. Zeke, you can crash in the guest room. I'll stay out here with Kukiro and make sure she doesn't go anywhere." He looked at her on the couch and gave a little wink.

"Very funny," Kukiro muttered as she was drifting off slowly. They all eventually manage to get to sleep.

Jak was still out cold in Toshi's bed. She wasn't moving but her face was showing pain in her head. All she could hear was: 'I'm coming back for you. I'm coming back for you. I'm coming back for you. I'm coming back for you. I'm coming back for you. I'm coming back for you. I'm coming back for you. I'm coming back for you'. JAK! Jak shot up awake as if from a terrible nightmare. She was covered in sweat and was disoriented, not realising where she was at first. Everything felt unfamiliar to her, her heart racing, fear running through her entire body, the last thing she remembered was the face of the creature up close to hers, then darkness. Was it all a dream? Was it real? Did it take me if it was? It was still dark out and it was pitch black in the room; she couldn't make anything out. She placed her hand at her side then felt a body. She jumped and nearly let out a scream but realised after her eyes started to adjust to the darkness, that it was Triss. She felt a rush of relief. It must have been a dream, she thought, calming herself down. She laid back down to go back to sleep but as soon as she closed her eyes, she saw the face again, she tried opening her eyes again but couldn't. She tried thinking to herself that it is just a dream. 'You are pure of heart; I wonder how long it would take to break you. I'm coming back for you.' The creature kept repeating these words, then all of a sudden; darkness, apart from one beam of light shining over Jak. The words kept repeating, 'You are pure of heart, I wonder how long it would take to break you. I'm coming back for you'. She put her hands over her ears trying to block out the words but to no avail, they just kept getting louder and louder to the point of shouting. His deep voice booming throughout the empty void around her.

"It's just a dream" she repeatedly kept whispering to herself, trying to snap out of it. The words kept coming, louder and louder. 'You are pure of heart, I wonder how long it would take to break you. I'm coming back for you.' JAK! Her head jolted up and she was face to face with the creature. She was caught off guard and she nearly fell backwards but she just managed to keep her balance.

Silence. Silence filled the void as the creature and Jak stared each other down. Jak was paralyzed with fear and so didn't move. "Am-am I… dreaming?" Jak asked, barely able to get her words out. The creature circled her, not breaking the line of sight. He then chuckled.

"Yes, and no; we are in your subconscious but trust me, I am very real."

"Who are you?" she asked, defensively. She was keeping her guard up. The creature paused for a moment, then responded.

"I am Akuma and I know what you are thinking, why am I here? What do I want?" Jak seemed a little taken aback but then realised if he can project himself into her mind, he could probably read it too. Akuma let out another chuckle. "On the grand scheme I want to enslave all of you mortals, to control the world and let it burn if I so choose but here in your mind? Well, you make me curious. In my infinite lifetime, I have met many humans but none are like you. When I held you I could feel your thoughts. You were more concerned about your friends than yourself, even though you were in immediate danger. I scanned your friends' thoughts, and they were only for themselves. Only one was concerned about you, the Asian one, Toshi was it? As for Kukiro, well as she is part of the Fallen Lotus clan, she has protective wards shielding her thoughts from me." He paused again and took a deep breathe. "I predict you will tell the others about our meeting tonight but I must warn you, that is a very bad idea. You are lucky you intrigue me; when I invade the mind, I can twist and warp, driving the most headstrong person insane. If you should tell them, I will tear you apart…" Akuma and his voice faded into the darkness and could not be seen any more, Jak suddenly shot up and awoke. It was daytime and Triss had already woken up and left the room.

She could hear them talking outside in the living room. She was thinking about telling them what she heard but she kept having the warning run through her mind. 'I will tear you apart.' It gave her chills just thinking about it. Against her better judgment, she heeded the warning and did not mention about Akuma. She left the room. As soon as she opened the door and everyone stared at her, they all stood up to give her a hug, all asking if she was okay and how she was feeling. She pretended to be fine as best as she could. She didn't know whether or not they believed her or they could tell she didn't want to talk about it but they didn't press any further.

Kukiro was up and about now. Her ribs were still sore but she could work through the pain now. As they all sat back down, she remained standing. "I need to go to the temple to see my masters and inform them of the situation. They will be able to guide me on what to do next." Toshi stood up immediately.

"You are not going anywhere without us; we are in this together." Kukiro smiled.

"I wasn't leaving without you. I want you all to come with me for your protection. The temple grounds are warded off to prevent evil spirits walking on the sacred ground; we can protect you there. You three, head back to your hotel rooms and pack your things, meet us back here in one hour. Toshi, I'll help you pack." They all nodded and immediately set off to the hotel to get their things. Toshi pulled Kukiro closer.

"Kukiro, I want to go with you but you need to tell me

what is going on. You need to explain to me how you knew this was real and how you do all the things you do." Kukiro shied away, trying to find the words.

"Not yet," she finally responded. "I promise I will tell all of you but we need to get Jak to safety." Toshi's ears pricked.

"Why Jak?" intrigued why her specifically and concerned for his friend.

"It was last night. She should be dead. Whenever a creature like Akuma singles someone out and spares them, it is never good. We need to get her to a safe space."

Toshi and Kukiro packed up some clothes and essentials. Travelling light, they headed downstairs to meet Jak, Zeke and Triss. As they exited the building, the three were in a car waiting. Zeke was in the driver's seat, Triss and Jak in the back seat. He turned to Kukiro and wound down his window. He flashed a salute and in a Scottish accent asked, "Where to Cap'n?" She opened the driver's door.

"I'll drive, you get in the back, Toshi you're up front, with me." Zeke looked disappointed but then smiled.

"Fine, this means I can nap!" He clambered onto the back seat and the group set off on their journey. As they set off, Triss leaned forward.

"So, where is this temple we are going to?" Kukiro keeping her eyes on the road, replied,

"Kurikoma. It's north of Miyagi; it's nearly a six-hour drive." Triss sat back, trying to think about what she could do for six hours. She leaned forward again.

"What if Akuma attacks us?"

"He won't. Akuma is a shadow Oni; he would be too weak during the day to do anything." Triss, relaxed by Kukiro's answer, sat back and looked out of the window, getting comfy for the journey ahead.

Toshi leaned in and whispered to Kukiro, "Is that true?" so as not to cause a stir. She looked in the rear-view mirror and saw no one was looking and she shook her head. Truth is, she hadn't seen a demon like this before. His power could be limitless.

The group had got about halfway through their journey to Kurikoma. It had mostly been a quiet trip, all of them tired but struggling to sleep. Whether it was that they were unable to find comfort being in a car, or their thoughts weighing heavily on their minds along with everything that had gone on, or whether they were unable to comprehend the reality of the situation and they were contemplating whether or not their lives would ever be the same.

Toshi could see everyone was fatigued, so had an idea. He looked at Kukiro. "So Kukiro, I believe you told us would explain everything to us, as to how you are the badass you are?" The groups' ears all pricked up in synchronisation and all focused on Kukiro awaiting her response. She glanced around for a second, making sure to stay focused on the road. She seemed nervous about talking about it but let out a sigh.

"I guess I did promise you. I don't know who my parents are. I was given to the Order of the Fallen Lotus when I was a baby; I grew up there. They taught me martial arts, how to use weapons and various techniques. I was selected to be part of a team. We were known as the 'yami no tenshi', or 'Angels of Light'. The order was created to combat the forces of evil that are hell-bent on world domination or destruction; we are keepers of the peace. Once we are designated as ready, we get posted around different parts of the world to guide and protect those who cannot know the existence of the team. I was sent to Tokyo alone as I tended not to work well with others." Kukiro looked at Toshi and the others to try and gauge their reactions; they seemed confused. She continued, "I was eager to prove myself. I posted up in the museum as there are a lot of artefacts. I wanted to see if there were any that were holding Onis but with no luck. Every night, I would wander the streets to find any activity but there was none; it was a dead-zone. I gave up searching shortly after meeting Toshi." She gazed at him and gave him a smile. "He showed me a kindness and love I had not felt before, so I decided my time would be better served putting effort into my own personal life but this was against the will of the order."

Triss leaned in. "That doesn't explain how you knew to come to the apartment after we had opened the scroll."

Kukiro nodded. "You are quite right. Toshi had explained to me about his life with you guys and what you did, so when I saw you three in his office, it piqued my curiosity and I thought you may have found something." Jak had a penny drop in her mind.

"That's why you came to the apartment that night, to look at the scroll!" Kukiro looked down, almost full of shame.

"Yes, I managed to sneak a look at it whilst you were in the bathroom and Toshi was in the kitchen. I made an excuse to disappear for a sec and went through your bag. I do apologise." Jak just waved it off.

"Don't worry about it; you saved me from Akuma." Zeke turned to Jak.

"How do you know his name? You were unconscious?" Jak nervously looked around, everyone looking to her for an answer. Crap! she thought, trying to think of an answer quickly.

"I was in and out for a bit. I heard him say his name," Jak responded, looking at everyone to see if they believed her; her heart thudding through her ribcage. They seemed to back off and finally said okay. Jak quickly changed the subject. "So as you were saying Kukiro." Kukiro looked befuddled, as if she forgot what they were originally talking about. Just as quickly as she'd forgotten, she remembered.

"Ah yes! As I pulled the scroll out of the bag, I saw what it was. I wanted to return it to the temple but before I could stash it in my coat the bathroom door opened, so I put it back in your bag. I planned to return later that night. However, by then it was too late. You know the rest as you were all there!"

They all seemed in awe about Kukiro. She really wanted to prove herself and be her own person. They admired her tenacity and drive, to complete the task ahead. "Any way guys, you should all get some rest, we still have a fair journey ahead. You will need your strength for when we have to walk." Triss almost leapt up out of her seat.

"Walk? Why would we walk if we have a car?!" Kukiro looked at her through the rear-view mirror and chuckled.

"We can't reach it by car; it wouldn't be a secret if you could, would it?" Triss fell back, slumped to her seat and let out a huff.

"I have the wrong shoes for this," she said, looking down at her knee-high, high-heeled boots. The group all had a laugh about it then, one by one they collapsed; their minds at ease for the time being.

'I'll tear you apart. I'm coming back for you, I'll tear you apart. I'm coming back for you, I'll tear you apart. I'm coming back for you, JAK!' Jak abruptly woke up in a panic, breathing heavily, covered in sweat and disorientated. "Jak! We are here!

Come on, shake a tail feather!" It was Zeke seeming flushed with excitement. Jak looked around. The car was empty; everyone was outside waiting for her. She stepped out of the car and squinted, her eyes adjusting to the bright lights of day. They seemed to be standing in a clearing of what seemed to be an expansive forest. The car was parked on the edge of the clearing. "Are you sure the car will be safe here?" Zeke asked. He loved this car, it'd been his favourite part of the trip; driving this car. Kukiro laughed, looking at him stroking the car as if it were a puppy.

"It will be fine, there are fences surrounding the entire forest covered with warning signs. There is only one entrance, which the order know about."

Zeke still looked concerned but decided to trust Kukiro. He kissed the car's bonnet and whispered goodbye, to which the group all chuckled and they started to follow Kukiro through the woods. It was peaceful, no cars, no voices; the only sounds were that of nature. The gentle breeze rolling through the trees rustling their leaves, birds chirping, it was magical; almost as if ripped from a work of art as nothing was out of place.

Most of them managed to keep pace with Kukiro, apart from Triss who was trailing behind. "Guys wait for me! My heels keep getting stuck in the ground!" she yelled, breaking the serenity of the forest. Zeke turned round, gave her his bag and picked her up to give her a piggyback. Amazingly, he still managed to keep pace with everyone despite the extra weight, at least for a good fifteen minutes down the path. Then he had to stop to rest.

"Kukiro, you guys go ahead I'll catch up." Kukiro took off her bag and sat down next to Zeke.

"We are sticking together," she said, giving him a warming smile. As they sat for five minutes, they all had some water and some rice cakes that Kukiro had packed in her sack. Toshi had prepared them before they left.

After they had finished their snacks and had some rest, they pushed forward. Triss walked and everyone slowed down a bit so she could keep up, much to the dismay of Kukiro. Not in a mean way; she was concerned as they hadn't yet reached the temple and Akuma could be round the corner waiting to strike but she knew it was better they stuck together. As they progressed up a steady slope, they reached another clearing. However, this one held a grand temple before them, the grounds spread as far as the eye could see. How this could stay hidden was beyond any of the group. The walls stood high and thick, the gates were solid wood and on the front was the crest of the Fallen Lotus. They had finally arrived at what Kukiro called 'home'.

Chapter 4

They entered the temple grounds, Kukiro breathing a sigh of relief that they were finally safe from Akuma's wrath. Although, she was still trying to hide the lie she had told the group, and so didn't let them see the relief on her face. As they entered, Kukiro lead the group. They all noticed the members were dressed in traditional outfits and that they all were whispering and staring at them. It must be because they were strangers who had entered the sacred temple. Most of them, however, were looking at Kukiro, bewildered that she would break one of the sacred rules: Never lead outsiders into the temple, lest you compromise the order.

They continued down the centre of the courtyard, with the building of traditional architecture surrounding them. Ahead was a larger building with magnificent steps leading up to the entrance that was miraculous. Walking around this place made them feel as though they had been transported back in time. There was no sense of any life outside the temple.

Upon starting up the steps, they saw two men coming down to meet them halfway: an elderly gentleman with longer, silver hair and a well-maintained beard. He also had a noticeable scar across his left eye. The second was a younger man with similar features, except his hair was jet black and he didn't have a beard. Perhaps they were relatives? Or was it just a coincidence. Either way, the younger man looked very displeased, whereas the elderly man seemed just a little confused. As they met in the middle, Kukiro dropped to her knees as if in prayer. "Grandmaster Hasashi, I seek your counsel and protection for my friends." The young man immediately drew his sword and pointed it at Kukiro.

"You traitor! How dare you address the Grandmaster after breaking one of our most sacred laws, compromising our Order's very existence! You and your friend should be put to death for this insolence-" Before he could continue, the old man raised his hand and placed it on the sword, pushing it away from Kukiro.

"Takeda, you will restrain yourself. Kukiro is still one of us and I am sure she has a good reason for bringing them here. Please show our guests to the dining quarters and make sure they are fed, then you will take them to the sleeping quarters and find them some beds." The young one, Takeda, immediately sheathed his blade. He bowed.

"Please forgive me, Grandmaster, I have stepped over the line." He stood upright and looked at the group. "You four, follow me, the dining quarters are this way." They were hesitant to follow at first, considering what Takeda had just said but still followed, cautiously.

"Rise Kukiro," the Grandmaster said, offering a hand to her. She didn't take it but instantly rose. "So, tell me what brings you all this way and why have you brought strangers here?" She looked around and saw people staring at them.

"Let's do this inside." They entered the huge structure and the large gates shut behind them.

"I want to apologise for my behaviour." Takeda said to the group. "It's just I have seen what has happened before when outsiders have come here and I don't want to risk the lives of our order." The others exchanged looks.

"It's okay, I understand it can be hard to trust again," Toshi said, putting his hand on Takeda's shoulder.

"What happened last time?" Zeke asked.

"A man came to our temple. He looked lost and afraid, we gave him food and shelter and sent him in the direction of the nearest town. He came back with friends during the night and raided our temple; he stole valuables and killed many of our men." Takeda looking down, showing pain in his face, remembering. "I was just a kid at the time but my brother was fighting; he lost his life." Triss looked heartbroken by the story.

"I am so sorry, Takeda," she exclaimed.

"Yeah man, that can't have been easy," Zeke added. "Trust me when I say we mean you no harm." Takeda looked up to four smiling faces.

"Thank you, I appreciate your kind words." Jak was looking around. There were so many people here living secluded from the world.

"If this place is so secure, how can it have so many people? Surely other people must know about it?" Jak enquired.

"I can see why you would think that but the road is well hidden," Takeda responded. They took a left and entered a building that was a grand hall, tables all lined up, each one seating four, spanning from one end of the hall to the other. Constantly going back and forth, were the other members of the Fallen Lotus, all greeting each other, greeting Takeda as they walked past. Some even greeted the group, though most just walked past them not even giving them a second glance. They sat down and almost immediately they were served rice and chicken with a katsu sauce and glass of sakura tea to wash it down.

"So, you want to know about the people?" Takeda enquired, as he could see they were powering through their food as if they hadn't eaten in days. Jak finished her mouthful.

"Yes, for a secret order, there must be a couple of hundred people here." Takeda took a small mouthful and finished it.

"Well, most of the people are orphans. We find the ones with the most potential and bring them here; others find out about us the hard way. Usually, they have encountered a demon and want help; others lose someone to the demon. We don't offer them to come with us though, they ask us." As he finished, he started drinking his tea.

Zeke, who had devoured his meal and drank his tea in that time, leaned in. "So Kukiro, she was an orphan?" Takeda stopped drinking immediately, cup still to his lips. He pulled it away as he looked confused.

"She didn't tell you?" All of them shook their heads. "Figures, she doesn't like talking about it but I figured if you guys were close enough for her to bring you here, she would have said something. Yes, she is an orphan but not when the Grandmaster first met her." Zeke looked confused.

"How do you mean?"

"Well, this was before Grandmaster Hasashi was who he is today. He was a veteran, he had taken on many Oni and saved a lot of lives. He met them on mission. Word had got out about an Oni in Kyoto." He paused to have another bite. "Her father was originally a member of the order; her mother too.

48

That was how they met. They left with good grace after finding out they were going to have Kukiro and reached out to Hasashi when they heard about the Oni. Kukiro must have been about two or three at the time. He slayed the Oni and was sitting down with them for a meal before he returned. However, that's when the second one attacked." Jak and Zeke gasped. Triss choked on a mouthful of rice. "It was like nothing Hasashi had ever faced before. It's how he got that scar. The Oni killed Kukiro's parents, then left, disappeared without a trace and nothing has been heard from it since."

There was silence from the group, only the voices around them and the clinking of cutlery on dishware could be heard. Toshi looked in shock. "That's why she was so persistent about finding them, to find the one that killed her parents." It all made sense: her tenacity, her ferociousness; she wanted revenge. "Anyway, Hasashi vowed to look after Kukiro. He was always harder on her for training than the other recruits, he was so proud when she reached the top of her class. But then she left straight after. She was meant to remain on the temple grounds until further instructions. Usually if you were to leave, you would not be allowed to come back but Hasashi knew why, so when he became Grandmaster, he discarded that rule."

The group, having finished their meal, headed to the sleeping quarters and they were given their own room, five bed rolls laid on the floor. As they were unpacking their things, Zeke turned to Takeda. "So what is your story? Orphan?" Takeda laughed. "No, me and my brother were born here. I think you can guess who my father is?" They all looked at each other, not wanting to say anything in case they were wrong. "You are the son of Hasashi?" Jak spoke up, taking the plunge.

Takeda nodded. "His wife, my mother, passed away giving birth to me. He always looked at me as the last gift he ever received from her, then when my brother died in the attack, he decided he didn't want me to risk anything going out hunting Oni, so he swore me into the guard and when he passes, I will take over as Grandmaster."

"Well, that's nice, at least you know he cares for you." Takeda looked down.

"Yes, I suppose, it's just that I have never seen what life is like beyond the walls. I was looking forward to the day I could venture outward to see the world! But it never came." Jak walked over and gave him a hug.

"Why not go ask him? If you don't ask, you will never find out." Takeda felt comfort within the hug but then stepped back.

"I have before, he always forbids it." Jak grabbed his shoulder.

"Well maybe you should do it anyway! Be true to you, not to anyone else. Besides, he may be upset at first but he will come to understand. He is worried about losing you. He isn't going to cast you aside because of you wanting to see the world or even living a different life!"

"It's not that simple, it never will be." Takeda turned to walk away. Jak grabbed his shoulder again and turned him back around.

"It's not simple because you are making it more difficult than it is. Life isn't about subjecting yourself to others, it's about taking risks for the things you want, doing things that you decide are right for you."

Takeda placed his hand on hers. Maybe she was right, he thought. He was filled with confidence again to take the plunge and talk to his father about it; he wouldn't want to risk losing his son over this.

Kukiro entered the bunks. She just put a bag down, not unpacking, and instantly turned to Jak and Takeda. "Jak, Tak, can you guys come with me? We need to go speak to the Grandmaster." Jak was taken aback.

"Me? Just me? Why not the others too?" She was panicking, why would they only want her? Did she do something wrong? She couldn't have, she has been doing the same as everyone else. She calmed herself down. I'm just overthinking again she said to herself.

They entered the building where they had left Kukiro and Hasashi before. He was sitting down on a cushion on the ground, cross legged with a small table in front of him with a bottle of Sake and four small cups. On the other side of the table there were three cushions for each of them to sit on. Jak sat in between Kukiro and Takeda, her heart pounding, feeling the pressure but not sure as to why. "Sake?" The Grandmaster offered holding up the bottle. Jak respectfully declined. He then poured one for himself, Kukiro and Takeda. "So Jak, tell me about your dream."

Crap!

Jak internally screamed to herself, how does he know? "Dream? What dream?" She decided to play ignorance, it may not be what she was thinking. The Grandmaster laughed.

"Come now Jak, the dream of Akuma? If you are worried about his threats don't worry, you will be quite safe here. You are on sacred blessed ground; if he were to turn up, he would be powerless." Jak, still nervous, couldn't find the words to speak. "Please Jak, myself and the Fallen Lotus wish to help you. Kukiro told us about the encounter with the Oni and the fixation he had with you but we need to know why." Jak looked at Kukiro to see if she agreed that she should share this information. Kukiro saw the desperation in her eyes, she simply nodded, then Jak exhaled heavily.

"O-OKAY, so he came into my dreams…" She went on to explain what had happened, what he had told her and the threats he had made to her. She actually felt relieved that it was all out in the open, until she saw the Grandmaster's face; he looked very concerned. He too had never seen such behaviour from an Oni and alongside Kukiro's testament, it made it all the more troubling.

"Thank you for that Jak, you may return to your friends. Please do not worry about the threats - you are very safe here," the Grandmaster said, trying to look reassuring but Jak could still the concern in his eyes. She did as he said and left the building promptly, leaving Kukiro, Takeda and Hasashi to deliberate. They caught Takeda up to speed on what happened. "Now that everyone is up to speed, firstly I want say, 'Well done Kukiro', you did the right thing bringing them here. I know it is usually against our order but it was the right thing to do." He nodded approvingly in her direction. "Takeda, I want you on guard duty round our guests, make sure they are safe. I fear that this Oni is more powerful than we can imagine; he may be able to break through the ward." Takeda looked concerned.

"How am I supposed to defend them? Our usual blades seem to have no effect on him?" The Grandmaster handed him a piece of paper.

"Go to the weaponsmith, ask him to complete the special order and imbue them with this." Takeda didn't look at the paper, he simply took it, bowed and headed to the blacksmith.

Grandmaster then turned to Kukiro. "I have a special task for you. I need you to travel to Mount Hachimantai, west of the Appi Springs, do you know of where I speak?" Kukiro nodded.

"The original home of the Fallen Lotus."

"Good, you remember my stories. Inside the temple behind the wooden statue is a secret entrance, go and recover the contents. Take the car you travelled here in; we will make a clearing for you to get the car direct to here."

Kukiro stood up and bowed, then proceeded to begin her journey to the mountain. However, she stopped in the doorway. Hasashi looked up. "Grandmaster, I wish to take my friends and Takeda with me. They have experience in finding the hidden entrances and I know Takeda would want to venture out; plus, he is in charge of keeping them safe." The Grandmaster thought about this for a minute.

"Your friends may accompany you but Takeda must stay." Kukiro looked to respond but the Hasashi shot her this look saying that he was no longer going to entertain the idea of his son leaving. She nodded and left, deciding to take matters into her own hands.

She entered the bunk to find all of them sitting around chatting. They all looked at her as if to see if she was okay. "Guys, grab your things, we need to head out." They all seemed very confused, after all, they had just arrived somewhere they thought was safe. Takeda was the first to say,

"What is going on? I was told to watch them and now you are taking them away from this place?" Kukiro, understanding the confusion, walked up to him and put her hand on his shoulder.

"You are coming too genius." Takeda couldn't believe

what he was hearing; he was being allowed to leave? After all these years, he can go outside the temple walls. No, it couldn't be, he thought to himself, something isn't right.

"So, Grandmaster Hasashi himself said that I was allowed to leave on this mission with you?"

Kukiro hesitated for a moment. "Yes, I convinced him that you would be beneficial to our team. He was sceptical at first but then agreed." She was trying her best to sell this, as she knew Takeda knew about how the grandmaster felt about him leaving. Takeda was apprehensive about the response he received. He could tell she was lying but he decided to roll with it. This would be his chance to venture out and prove to his father that he has nothing to worry about. He smiled and nodded.

The group packed light and proceeded back out through the front gate. Takeda turned back and saw Hasashi looking out to the gate; Takeda quickly turned and left. Hasashi wasn't surprised. When they were younger, Kukiro and Takeda used to always sneak out; he just prayed that Takeda would be safe. The group of now six, went back to the car. Unfortunately, they realised they wouldn't have enough room for all of them. "What do we do now? Can we walk it?" Zeke asked. Kukiro shook her head.

"It would take a few days to walk the distance, we need to take the vehicle." Jak took the keys from Zeke.

"I will take this into town and trade it for something bigger." Zeke looked in horror.

"Not my baby! There must be another way!"

"For all of us to go we need a bigger car. Takeda, you ride with me, the rest of you meet us at the edge of the road in an hour," Jak replied, getting into the driver's side. They sped off to deal with the task at hand, Triss putting her arm round Zeke who was clearly upset.

"Chin up big guy, it was only a car." Zeke sighed.

"I know, I just didn't get to say goodbye." Kukiro, Toshi and Triss laughed as they all headed towards the main road.

Almost an hour and a half passed and there was still no sign of Jak or Takeda; Kukiro was starting to worry. Pacing up and down, there were no sounds of any cars in the distance, just the silence and the rustling of trees in the breeze. So many thoughts were racing through her mind: Did they get into trouble? Are they stranded? Did they run into Akuma? So many worries flowing through at once. She started hyperventilating, Toshi noticed and immediately stood up and took her hands to bring her in close. He whispered, "They are fine, it's Takeda's first time out of the Temple. Jak is probably just showing him a few things whilst they are there."

He was probably right, she thought, taking a deep breath in and exhaling, calming down and relieving the stress in her mind. Another ten minutes passed and they spotted the two coming up the road in an SUV with an elongated boot, essentially a pickup truck with a roof. Both of them were smiling and absolutely fine, much to the relief of Kukiro. As they pulled up, she went to them rather rapidly. "What took so long?" she demanded rather aggressively. Jak pulled back as if offended.

"Sorry, it took a while to find the right vehicle. Calm down." Kukiro realised how aggressive she was being and took another deep breath, then she responded,

"I'm sorry, I was just worried, especially as Akuma could be around anywhere and with the interest he has in you Jak…" Jak put her hand on Kukiro's shoulder.

"It's fine, I get why you are worried, I am sorry it took so long." They both smiled at each other. Triss stepped in between them.

"Hate to break up the lovers' quarrel but we are on a time scale correct? Let's pack our stuff up and hit the road!" They all started packing. Zeke was still looking upset and Toshi was counting the seats.

"Hey Jak? You know this can only seat four?" Jak smiled.

"Way ahead of you, Tosh!" She pulled out from the cabin some blankets and cushions which she laid out in the roofed flatbed. "You and Kukiro can chill in the back!" she added with a little wink.

Kukiro blushed and looked at Toshi, who smiled nervously, also blushing. So, they made their way to the original Fallen Lotus temple, hoping to find the answers they sought. "Kukiro, where should I go?" Jak said upfront, putting on her seatbelt.

"Head to Appi Springs. When we arrive, we walk. Be careful, it's getting dark and Akuma will come looking for you," Kukiro responded, before hopping onto the flatbed with Toshi. Jak nodded and set off on the journey, keeping an eye to the sky in case he did turn up.

They were a few hours in and Jak was falling asleep at the wheel. Her and Takeda swapped with Zeke and Triss, in order to get a few hours' rest before they arrived. Toshi and Kukiro were snuggled up in the blankets with each other, fast asleep. Zeke and Triss were wide awake after having a few hours rest in the first part of the trip. Zeke turned to Triss, speaking softly so as not to wake them. "So your attitude towards Kukiro has changed, have you stopped trying to pursue Toshi now?" Triss looked at him with eyes of regret.

"Yes, I guess I was just upset that he moved on, maybe wanting what I can't have? It was just when I saw them together, there was a passion and love there that me and Tosh never had and honestly? I am happy for him, he deserves to be happy." Zeke looked almost proud.

"Aww look at little Triss, acting all grown up." She gave him a friendly punch on the arm and they both laughed, again softly so as not to wake anyone. "Seriously though, Triss, you have come so far, I am impressed how much you've matured about the situation."

They both looked at each other. A certain kind of silence was held, not an awkward one though, they just stared intently, both unable to take their eyes of each other. The truck started to swerve a little but Zeke quickly snapped out of it and corrected the direction. Triss did not take her eyes off him. He turned back and said, "Get some rest Triss, I will wake you when we arrive." Triss looked disappointed but let yet out a large yawn so decided he was right; she decided to have a rest too. So all but Zak were sleeping, as he took the friends to their destination.

Chapter 5

Jaaaaaak. Jaaaaaak. JAK WAKE UP!

Jak shot up awake, the voice in her head was that of Akuma. She looked around. It was still dark out but saw leaning over her was Zeke. "Wake up sleepy head, time for a leisurely stroll!" She groaned and rubbed her eyes, looking around she could only see Zeke, Toshi and Triss. She stepped out of the vehicle and looked around. The only source of light was coming from the moon high in the sky, reflecting off the damp ground and slush lumps, where crisp white snow used to be.

"Where's Kukiro and Takeda?" she asked, still groggy from just being woken up so suddenly. Toshi offered her some water and some cooked chicken.

"They went to scout ahead, she said that while Kukiro is a better scout, Takeda is a better swordsman and still actually has his blade." Jak thought that was fair enough and proceeded to eat a little bit of chicken and took a small mouthful of water.

Emerging from the shrubbery to the west, Takeda signalled for them to come over. As they approached Takeda, they realised Kukiro was not with her. Before they could ask, Takeda spoke. "Kukiro is up ahead. She sent me to retrieve you guys, the path forward is clear, she is going to continue ahead scouting but be within earshot of us in case anyone falls into danger." They all nodded, acknowledging Takeda and all carried on. The mountains were quiet, the group were very quiet, they wanted to stay quiet so as not to alert anyone to their presence, assuming there was someone to alert.

As they progressed to the temple, Kukiro appeared. She signalled for them to stop moving, then for Takeda to come over. There were hushed words being spoken, Jak and the others couldn't make out what they were saying, Takeda came back to the others with Kukiro. "What is going on?" Jak asked, noticing the serious look on their faces, still maintaining a hushed tone. Takeda was the first to respond.

"We are close to the temple, about five minutes out. However, Kukiro has scouted ahead and noticed people have set themselves up in there. We are going to go in, take the guards out and do a sweep through, you need to stay here in the shadows in case anyone passes through." All of them looked concerned about this information. Zeke chimed up.

"Who are they?" Kukiro answered this time.

"I am not sure. They have weapons, most likely a small-time gang; they shouldn't be too much trouble." The group split up. Kukiro and Takeda headed to the temple to clear it out while Toshi, Jak Triss and Zeke hid in the shadows to wait for the all-clear.

About ten minutes went passed and no sign of either Takeda or Kukiro was given to the others. However, a crack of snapping twigs under a foot resonated from the opposite direction. The group hid behind some trees and laid down in some bushes. A light was coming from that direction too; a flashlight, nearly catching them out. It was one man, armed, most likely on patrol. They didn't have a way to warn Kukiro and Takeda. Jak was panicking as were Toshi and Triss, if they couldn't get a warning out to them it could put them in serious danger. Zeke however, seemed calm and collected. They saw why: he was gripping his rebar ready to strike, when the man reached their position and started going passed, Zeke snuck up behind him. As he was about to strike a branch snapped, the man turned around, he reached for his weapon but it was too late. Zeke readjusted his strike and smacked the rebar clean against his temple, rendering the man unconscious.

Zeke then dragged his body to the tree line, out of sight in case there were any others on patrol in the area who might have heard the scuffle; luckily no one else turned up. A good fifteen minutes passed before Kukiro and Takeda returned. They noticed the unconscious man on the ground. He had a large gash where the rebar impacted and dragged along his scalp, blood was dripping down his face. They looked at the group. "Who took him out?" Takeda asked. Zeke, looking proud of himself, held the rebar in his hand as if a baseball bat was in its place.

"That would be me." Takeda looked approving, Kukiro however was looking at the wound.

"He is bleeding-out, we need to help the wound. Quickly, Tak, Zeke, pick him up and carry him to the temple, you know where to put him Tak." He nodded, then he and Zeke took him to the temple, the others following behind keeping an eye out for more patrols.

They arrived at the temple grounds. It was less grand than where the Order was based now but that could be due to the lack of care in being abandoned, then overrun by thugs. The door was broken and splintered, almost rotting. The walls were cracked and the paint faded, the buildings didn't fare much better. One's roof had fully collapsed in, others had holes or simply no structural integrity, looking like a stiff breeze would bring them down. The courtyard had been lit up by torch sconces dotted around the grounds and there was a large fire pit in the centre. The group was led to a building to the right which seemed to be the most stable.

When they entered the building, they saw a large group of men, most still unconscious but all tied up. The ones who were awake were struggling to get free of their bindings; they had been gagged as well to prevent any unnecessary noise. They sat the injured man down and tied him up. They propped him upright in order for Kukiro to treat the wound. Jak pulled out a bottle of water from her bag and gave it to Kukiro. She tore some fabric from her sleeve, doused it with water and then poured some into the open wound, washing away some of the blood to have a look at what they were dealing with. It was a fairly small cut but deep enough to cause some serious bleeding. She placed the cloth against it, applying pressure to help stop the bleeding.

"Takeda, ask them if they have any medical supplies." He grabbed one of the conscious ones, he removed the gag and the thug began yelling in Japanese. Takeda simply slapped him across the face; he was more cooperative after that. He asked if they had any medical supplies, he received a response no one could understand except him and Toshi. He went to fetch the supplies. He came back with what looked like a medical supply box from a store or an office. He opened it up to find a stitching kit and some bandages. Kukiro proceeded to stitch up the wound and wrap bandages around his head.

"There, that should stop the bleeding and he should be

fine now…" She turned around and said to the man who was ungagged in Japanese, "When we leave, take him to a hospital and make sure his skull and brain are fine." He looked at the injured man and nodded. The group walked out, shutting the doors behind them.

"Right, so why are we here Kukiro? This is the old grounds for the Fallen Lotus," Takeda asked, clearly familiar with the history of the Order, most likely through the stories his father told Kukiro as well.

"The Grandmaster has asked me to get some things that were left here in a secret room behind a wooden statue." Zeke's eyes lit up like a child at Christmas time.

"More loot? Say no more, we are your guys!" Kukiro laughed and shook her head.

"These items are not for selling, they are to be returned to the Grandmaster." Zeke frowned and crossed his arms.

"Fine." They headed to the back building where the Grandmaster's chambers would have been. As they entered, they could see the door was smashed in, most likely by the gentlemen tied up in what used to be the dining quarters and the place had been stripped of anything valuable.

As they ventured further into the building, they saw the statue, although it could have been considered four. Four warriors each brandishing different weapons, were immortalised in these statues; possibly former Grandmasters, Jak thought. Her thought process was broken by Kukiro. "Right, so there should be a secret entrance behind them, everybody spread out and see if you can find the entrance." They each spread out to take a section of the wall, trying to see any sign of the entrance Kukiro mentioned. They spent about five minutes searching, before they each started to give up and sit down, thinking of ways to find this entrance. Jak however, was still standing at her section, looking it up and down intently. She realised when she was standing at a section with a faint breeze slipping through a crack, gently moving a few strands of her hair.

She moved to one of the wooden statues. She swept up some of the dust that had layered on top, then returned to door. Using her free hand, she had it hovered over the wall trying to feel the breeze. No luck. She then got the dust and gently sprinkled it across the wall, she then saw it get sucked into a small sliver. She focused on where it went in then followed it around, being careful not to lose the mark. She saw the outline of the door and as she backed out, she could still see it. She focused on it as she got more dust, not losing sight of the faint lines. She then rubbed the dust across the lines, marking out the doorway.

"Guys, I found the doorway." The defeated group sprung up with hope, all surrounding the sealed doorway. They all took turns trying to force it open but it wouldn't budge.

"Could we try busting it down?" Zeke suggested, holding his rebar at the ready.

"No, I know you can swing that thing hard but even you wouldn't be able to make more than dents in this wood," Kukiro informed. "There must be a mechanism that opens it, we need to search the entire building." However, as Kukiro mentioned that, Jak noticed something on the back of one of the statues. It looked almost like a button. She went up and pushed it; as she pushed the button a section of the statue's leg popped out with carved writing on it. She called Toshi over to come and read it.

"It's a puzzle. If entrance is what you seek then you must

solve this riddle: a shield will block a sword but will not block an axe, if the archer's aim is true however, the doorway will open to you."

They seemed perplexed by the puzzle. Looking around to see where the answer could be, Takeda was the first to look at the statues from the front. The four warriors were each holding a weapon — a sword, a shield, a battle-axe and a bow. "The statues, we have to move the statues!" he called out to everyone. They all reconvened. Triss looked up at them.

"How are we supposed to move these things? They must weigh a ton!" Takeda looked around the building. There were four wheels in each corner, each emblazoned with a weapon in the riddle.

"The wheels rotate the statues, quick everyone, get to a wheel, Jak you stay here and make sure the positioning is okay." Each went to a wheel, Toshi and Triss taking the same wheel.

"Okay, first we need to move the swordsman ninety degrees clockwise." Kukiro rotated the wheel. It was a struggle being that the mechanism was very old but once she got it going, the momentum carried the weight better. Once the swordsman was in position, Jak called out, "Okay, stop! Next the shield carrier needs a full one hundred and eighty to face the swordsman!" Zeke was up next. He was forcing it as much as he could but the wheel would not budge. He yelled.

"It won't move! Something must be blocking the turn." He was right, the axe wielder elbow was colliding with the shield.

"Okay stop a sec, Takeda move the axe wielder clockwise and keep going, Zeke once I say 'go' turn your wheel." Takeda started moving his wheel and similar to Kukiro, at first it was a struggle but then the momentum started carrying the weight.

"Okay Zeke, now." Zeke started turning the wheel, the building started to shake under the force of the two statues, splinters and small shards of timber from the roof began to fall.

"Takeda stop!" Jak called out, quickly realising what was happening. Takeda stopped. The building started to calm down, splinters and shards ceasing to fall.

The process continued. Zeke having the shield carrier blocking the swordsman and the axe wielder swinging at the shield carrier's back. The archer started turning. Once she was aimed at the axe wielder's head, a large clunking noise happened and as they returned to the doorway, they could see it had popped ajar. Zeke, Toshi and Takeda pulled the door open with all their might and they could see into a cave which led into the mountain. It was pitch black. Luckily Jak had her torch, so she led the way.

They moved down the tunnel for what seemed an eternity; there didn't seem to be an end to it. They couldn't even see the entrance behind them anymore. They pressed forward until they could see the tunnel getting wider and wider. Eventually, they were in a large, circular room with five sarcophagi evenly spread on the outside and a plinth on the centre; the plinth held a scroll. As they walked up to the scroll, Jak heard faint whispers. 'Jak, Jak, Jak, you told them'. It was Akuma's voice; she just brushed it off as her imagination.

Toshi picked up the scroll and began to read it. Everyone was nervous considering what happened the last time they read a scroll. 'Jak, you may be protected from me mentally, but I'll be coming for you.' She shook her head, trying to get rid of the voice. "Here lies the founders of the Fallen Lotus, may their legacy live forever in the hearts and minds of the future protectors." They noticed each sarcophagus had a weapon on top, bar one. There was a bow, an axe, daikatana and a razor-edged shield.

"That must be what we were sent to collect, everyone, grab the weapons," Kukiro instructed. Jak walked over to the fifth sarcophagus to inspect it. She noticed the outline of a weapon was carved onto the sarcophagus but it was too faded to see.

'I am coming for you Jak but first, I think I need to warm up, perhaps your friends?' Jak looked round at all her friends looking at all the weaponry: Zeke playing around with the battle-axe, Toshi holding the shield, Triss the bow and Kukiro with the daikatana. 'Are you ready to watch them all die before you? When I am through with them, you will be begging for death.' She was clutching her head, tears streaming down her face. She was being plagued with images of her friends dying, their bodies being twisted and mutilated by Akuma. "Stop, please." She fell to her knees. "Stop, stop, stop, stop, STOP IT NOW!" A hand grabbed her shoulder and she snapped back to reality, looking up at her friends with her bloodshot, teary, eyes. They were looking at her with worry.

"Stop what Jak?" Toshi asked. She couldn't believe that she'd said that out loud, she thought it was all in her head. She dried her eyes and stood up.

"It's nothing guys, let's just go." Takeda reached to her.

"Jak-" She pushed him away.

"I said I am fine!" she yelled angrily. She walked off back down the tunnel, flashlight in hand.

They reached the car. As the rest were packing up the weapons, Takeda pulled Jak forcefully to one side. This time she wasn't putting up a fight, she just went along with it. "Jak please talk to me, what happened in there? What did you want to stop?" she sighed.

"Please just let it go, it doesn't matter."

"It does to me, I care about you." He held her hand, she felt a flutter in her chest but she resisted it and freed her hand.

"I am fine, let's just go." She walked off with Takeda, got in the car and started engine. Takeda still stood in the same spot, was crushed. He truly thought she felt the same way and could open up to him, like he did to her. He returned to the car and the journey back was in silence.

Dawn was breaking as they reached the first clearing where they'd originally parked. However, now there was a path opened up to allow them to drive up. Jak followed the path for a while, when all of a sudden, they could see smoke through the gaps in the trees. They all looked up. It was coming from the temple. Takeda went ashen in the face before only uttering one word.

"Father…"

Chapter 6

The group approached the burning temple. The gate which previously had stood strong had been destroyed and was splintered inwards to the courtyard. The buildings remained mainly intact apart from scorch marks and smoke billowing from the fires which had already been put out. Those who were able-bodied, worked hard around the temple trying to clean up the temple grounds and prevent all the fires. They carried the injured to the sleeping quarters where they were being treated for their wounds. As the six entered the grounds, there were all too familiar claw marks on some of the walls. Akuma had attacked the grounds.

They disembarked from the vehicle. Takeda and Kukiro ran to help the others, whereas Jak, Toshi, Zeke and Triss looked at the devastation around them, guilt surrounding them as they felt this was their fault, for reading the scroll. They collected themselves, decided to do right by the group and help them. Triss and Jak were helping collect the injured, whilst Toshi and Zeke helped stop the burning and helped with the clean-up.

As Takeda and Kukiro brought another injured man in, Takeda noticed at the other end of the building a man with bandages, cloth rolled around his chest and part of his face. But he noticed the white beard poking out, albeit more red than white now; it was the Grandmaster. Tears started swelling in Takeda's eyes as he realised who it was and immediately rushed over to him. Kukiro was nearly falling under the weight of the man but was able to steady herself. "Father? Father? What happened?" Takeda asked, sitting by Hasashi's side. He stirred, barely conscious, his visible eye almost rolling into the back of his head. Almost out of breath, he managed a few words.

"We… were… attacked." Before he could continue, he fell unconscious, succumbing to the painkillers he was given.

Takeda dropped his head and began to weep. Unable to contain it anymore, he was riddled with guilt. Kukiro came over, sat next to him and put her arms around him trying to bring comfort to the grieving son. "It's my fault," Takeda said in a solemn voice. Kukiro was taken aback. Why was Takeda blaming himself?

"Tak this isn't your fault, no one could have predicted this would have happened. They shouldn't have been able to stand on the temple grounds." Takeda looked up at her, teary eyed.

"I should have stayed, I could have helped, I could have stopped this." Kukiro stood up and picked him up.

"Don't do this to yourself Tak, you wouldn't have been able to change what happened. You yourself could have been hurt or worse, killed!" Takeda turned away, broken from this.

"I will never leave the temple again."

Kukiro decided to leave him to be with his father alone, Besides, the doctors and other injured, he also needed some space. A few hours passed, the smoking had stopped and the temple was calmer. Outside near the main gate were fifteen bodies, covered in blankets. They couldn't survive their injuries. The Order stood out in the courtyard with their heads bowed, saying prayers for the fallen. Jak, Triss and Zeke, were in the crowd whereas Takeda and Kukiro were at the front. A lot of tears were being shed; friends and family were lost.

After the prayers, members in the Order proceed to carry the bodies and bury them outside the grounds, where they had a graveyard so people can visit the fallen. Once they were buried, everyone gathered at the front of the Grandmasters building, looking for guidance on what to do. Takeda stood up to the task and addressed the group. "As you know, my father, Grandmaster Hasashi was injured severely during the attack. I will be assuming the role until he is fit to resume his position." There were murmurs and whispers among the crowd, doubting that he would be able to lead.

"Where were you during the attack?" someone from the crowd shouted. Takeda dropped his head, thinking about how things could have changed if he stayed.

"Kukiro, myself and the visitors were away on the Grandmaster's orders. I know you all do not think I am ready but I plan to do my very best. It will be a struggle but as long as we all work together, we can come back from this and prevail." There were more whispers and murmurs within the crowd again, still sceptical of Takeda leading. Kukiro could see the crowd was getting restless and agitated so ran up the steps and stood with Takeda.

"Guys I know you don't like the situation; no one does. We have been hit hard but we can't let this Order fall to shambles, we need to rise up and be strong. So we are going to rebuild what is broken and damaged and come back stronger."

The crowd were still unconvinced and dispersed either to work, to eat or to visit the injured; all bar four. Jak, Toshi, Trish and Zeke all stayed to help their friends in their time of need. Kukiro and Takeda walked down, almost defeated by their failure to rally the order but given hope, thanks to their friends. "Thank you for staying guys," Takeda said. He and Kukiro both bowed to them in respect. Zeke stepped forwarded.

"Enough formalities, we are friends. So what do you want us to do?" Both of them looked up, impressed by the enthusiasm.

"First we need to rebuild the gate. Zeke, start chopping down some trees from the forest. Triss, go and assist the doctor with those still in his care. Toshi and Jak, use the truck to drag the trees in once they have fallen. You should be able to get chains from the blacksmith." They all nodded and assigned their tasks, they all set off to do their part. Takeda turned to Kukiro. "Thank you for your help." Kukiro smiled.

"It's okay, I am sorry neither of us could get the people to help. What should we do?" Takeda's thoughts were on his father. Wishing he could do something to aid his recovery, he didn't know what to do.

"I guess I will help Zeke getting those trees down, you try talking to the people individually to see if they will help; this is their home too and I'm sure they will come around." Kukiro nodded in agreement and set off to talk to the people and Takeda left to join Zeke in getting the lumber they need to rebuild.

As the day passed to evening the small team worked without a break, Zeke and Takeda were covered in sweat and exhausted from cutting the trees down, then hooking them up to the truck for Jak and Toshi to bring into the grounds. Triss helped the doctor as much as she could: changing bandages, cleaning wounds to prevent infection and in general, providing comfort. Kukiro had no luck. The people of the Fallen Lotus had truly fallen. They were demoralised from the attack. Most didn't see Takeda as a leader so refused to listen, others just couldn't bring themselves to listen as they were still mourning those they had lost.

The exhausted team met up at the dining quarters to sit down for a meal and something to drink and to provide updates. Takeda led the meeting. "So, we managed to get twenty trees. We can use most for the new gates and what is leftover can be used for general repairs to the buildings. Zeke and Toshi, if you can start prepping them tomorrow morning, we can start putting the gates in place by the following day." They nodded in agreement. Takeda turned to Kukiro. "How did you get on? Any changes?" She shook her head.

"No luck. I will go round again tomorrow, see if I can convince them." Takeda looked down into his lap, feeling disappointed in himself.

"No, I will call a gathering in the courtyard and address them all. You help Zeke and Toshi, Jak you too, the more we get prepping the wood, the sooner we can feel less exposed." Again, both nodded in agreement. The whole team were listening to him, taking his lead, giving him hope that he could convince the rest of the Fallen Lotus to help. He then turned to Triss. "How was it with the doctor? How are the patients doing?" Triss finished a drink.

"Everyone is in a stable condition, we are preventing infections by changing the dressings and cleaning out with water but we need alcohol to properly disinfect the wounds, and some require stitches." Takeda nodded.

"When our supply team go on a run in the morning, I will let them know to collect these as well."

Triss acknowledged the response. "I will let the doctor know. I am going to head back there before I rest to see if he needs anything else."

"Triss... how is my father?" Takeda asked. He hadn't stopped thinking about him all day and it was weighing heavily on his mind. She looked down, unable to make eye contact with Takeda.

"Not great, he is still unconscious and is not showing signs of improvement but he isn't deteriorating, so that's a positive." Although Triss had tried to spin a positive on it, Takeda just went quiet, still feeling guilty. Jak placed her hand on his leg.

"He is a fighter Jak, he will pull through." Those words brought little comfort to him but still he put on a smile, appreciating the effort.

The next day was a struggle as most of the team were still fatigued from the day before. Measuring and cutting the trees was a massive struggle. By the time the midday sun had reached its peak, they were just about ready to collapse. They took a short break to rehydrate and rest their arms from the sawing. As they continued after their limited rest, Takeda noticed that most of the people were watching them. He composed himself and stood by them, ready to make another attempt at rallying them. "You see? You see what we do? We are trying whereas you don't. Even those who have only been here for a few days are trying to help rebuild, yet you do nothing! The order is a community. We are brothers, sisters, lovers; we have stuck together through hard times! Why do you fail now?" They all looked blank, as if not interested in what he was saying or just not bothered.

"I am almost glad Grandmaster Hasashi is unconscious, his heart would break at the sight of this." Takeda shook his head in derision of the attitudes of the group and went to help his friends. They looked at Takeda, seeing the frustration taking over. There was a stunned silence throughout the temple. Most felt disrespected by the young leader but chose to ignore him and go about their day. However, one man approached them. He immediately dropped to his knees in front of Takeda, his hands and nose on the ground.

"Please forgive my ignorance, Grandmaster. Please allow me to assist you." Takeda looked at him, still frustrated but Jak came over and put her hand on his shoulder. He took a moment to breathe and calm down.

He helped the man to his feet and bowed in front of him. "There is nothing to forgive, please, we welcome the help." The man immediately bowed and went to Toshi and Zeke to see how he could help. Kukiro approached Takeda.

"You may not have inspired everyone, but it is a start." They smiled at each other and proceeded to get back to work. Over the next couple of days, they managed to get the gates replaced and fitted. After seeing that, more people joined to help restore the temple. A few were treating the wood for the gate to make sure it would maintain its integrity, others were working on the rooftops or cleaning up rubble and dirt. Eventually, the majority of the temple started to work together to bring the temple back to its former glory. A lot of the injured had started getting back up on their feet thanks to the doctor and Triss. Kukiro and Takeda stood at the top of the steps leading to the Grandmaster's building overlooking the entire temple grounds, admiring the work everyone was doing, proud of what they were managing to accomplish and that everyone was starting to finally come together.

"Look at what you accomplished Tak, you managed to get everyone to unite and work together. They have even accepted Jak, Zeke, Tosh and Triss as their own." Takeda did look proud but then turned to Kukiro.

"Not me; us. I could never have done this without yours or their support. This victory is yours just as much as it is mine." They both smiled at each other then turned back to notice Triss was sprinting up the stairs.

"Tak! Kukiro! Come to the sleeping quarters quick!" she shouted, still charging up the stairs.

"What's wrong?" Takeda yelled back. "It's your father, he is awake!" They both looked at each other then started powering down the stairs and raced to the sleeping quarters as fast as they could. As they entered, there was a small crowd round his bed. Both of them fought through to get the Hasashi. When they got through, they saw the man. No longer barely able to breathe but a strong healthy man, even though his ribs were still heavily bandaged, with a cloth wrapped around his damaged eye.

He noticed them almost immediately and asked everyone to give them privacy. Once cleared, he got out of bed, wincing a little from his torso and proceeded to give them a hug. "I am so glad you are all safe." Tak started tearing up.

"I am so sorry I left." His head dropped. Hasashi proceeded to lift his head and hold him.

"Don't be sorry Takeda, I am glad you did, you were safe away from here. If you were here you could have been seriously injured and I wouldn't have been able to live with myself if you did, because I would have been the one who kept you here." He turned to Kukiro and smiled. "You did the right thing." She quickly bowed. Hasashi returned to his bed and sat upright. "So, tell me what I have missed."

They updated him on the mission, the repairs and the problems they were having with the people. Hasashi was listening intently, taking in all the information, he was struggling as his torso was still in pain but he powered through. Once they finished debriefing him on the situation, he took a moment to think about what had happened. "Very well, I am glad everything worked out in the end. Once I am fully recovered, we will still have a lot to do and go through but enough for now. Rest and take the day for relaxing, you both have earned it. Meanwhile, I am going to get some sleep, I may have been unconscious for the past few days but I am still very tired."

They said their goodbyes and left Hasashi to rest. Once outside, Kukiro turned to Takeda. "Do you think we should have asked what happened?" Takeda had the same thought.

"No not yet. We can wait until he is fully recovered." Kukiro agreed; reliving the traumatic events of that night wouldn't be good for the Grandmaster's recovery. They went to Jak, Triss, Toshi and Takeda who were in the dining quarters having some lunch and sat down.

Triss was the first to notice them approaching, "How was he?" Takeda smiled.

"He is doing well, still sore but definitely much better. Thank you for your help with his recovery." Triss felt warmth from the gratitude and gave a soft smile. They all sat down properly for the first time in the past week: they ate, they drank, they laughed. It was as if for a moment, the problems they were facing didn't exist, they were just in the moment;

they felt carefree. By the time they left, it was almost midnight and they returned to their quarters for a good sleep.

"Jak, I know you can hear me." She stirred in her sleep. She hadn't heard that voice since before the attack. The deep raspiness however, was far too familiar. She shot up awake and started clutching her head. Finally awake, that voice wasn't inside her head. She turned and saw a shadowy figure standing over Kukiro and Toshi as they slept. It was not moving, just staring at them. His gaze suddenly fell upon Jak in almost an instant. She prepared to yell as loud as she could. "Ah, ah, ah, I wouldn't do that if I were you." He looked back down at Toshi and Kukiro. Jak wasn't sure what he was looking at but then there was a slight shimmer, reflecting off a blade hovering over the pair. She held in her breath. "Wouldn't want your friends to get seriously hurt now, would you? You have been a very naughty girl, Jak." She was still silent, not taking her eyes off the blade. "Relax, as long as you play along, your friends will live... for now." She looked at him, fear flowing through her body. She quickly nodded in agreement and Akuma retracted the blade, disappearing up his sleeve. "Very good. You like what I did with the place? I was disappointed you weren't here to see me in action. Now that I am at full strength, tearing this place apart was easy." Jak just let out a smile.

"You can't be that powerful, we have rebuilt and the Fallen Lotus is stronger than ever." He darted forward and grabbed her by the throat.

"You insignificant little worm. That was but a taste of my true power, I could turn this entire temple and its people to dust with a wave of my hand!" he said, filled with pure hatred and anger. He released her and calmed down again. "Besides, I want them alive. I want them to see." She seemed confused.

77

"See what?" she whispered, looking around making sure no one in the room was stirring. Akuma let out a little chuckle.

"Why would I tell you? Takes away the surprise. I will give you a clue, it is what anyone would need when conquering the world." She tried to think straight but was too focused on Akuma. "Not a clue? Shame, I thought that with anyone demon's blood would have more sense than that." She felt a chill run down her spine when she heard those words.

"Demon's blood? What do you mean?" Akuma looked shocked at first but then had a little chuckle again.

"You mean your wonderful Hasashi never told you? You have demon's blood in you, it's why I took an interest in you, I could smell it on you."

She thought back to that moment of their first encounter. He did smell her before she passed out; she hadn't even realised that they were not speaking aloud. It does explain the weird feelings she had when holding the scroll and blade. A sense of dread ran through her, questioning her very existence; who was she really? Why does she have this blood? Why didn't Grandmaster Hasashi tell her? She shook her head in denial. "You're lying, you're trying to manipulate me but it isn't going to work." Akuma just chuckled.

"What reason would I have to manipulate you? Do with that information what you will but for now I take leave, I will see you soon." He turned to the shadowy corner then looked back over his shoulder. "Real soon."

He faded away into the darkness and Jak was just sitting there, shaking, tears streaming down her face. She wanted to believe he was lying but Akuma was right; he had be no reason to manipulate her. She needed answers from Hasashi, so proceeded to leave her bed and head to his bed in the nursing ward. As she stepped outside a hand grabbed her shoulder. She started panicking and turned round to strike whoever it was but her hand was grabbed; it was Takeda.

"Whoa there fighter, calm down it's only me, is everything okay? You're shaking." She crumpled to her knees. Takeda, trying to slow her fall, joined her on the ground. She looked him in the eyes, hers bloodshot from the tears.

"I don't know anymore. I need to talk to Hasashi." She got up to go but Takeda held onto her.

"He is asleep, just like you should be, let's talk to him in the morning." She forced herself free from his grasp.

"No, it can't wait." Takeda followed her.

"I will go with you then." She turned and stopped him.

"No, I need to do it alone." Takeda stopped as she continued her walk to the ward. He was concerned so he decided to follow her in secret. He waited 'til he was out of her vision, then proceeded to the ward, using the night to his advantage.

Jak arrived at the ward. There were a couple of night nurses to watch over the patients but the doctors were resting. She headed to Hasashi to confront him. As she arrived by his side, his eyes opened and looked right at Jak. "I figured you would stop by. Draw the curtains; this will require some privacy." He signalled for the nurses to leave the building. As they left, Takeda snuck in and ducked between the beds, making his way across to Hasashi and Jak.

Hasashi gestured for Jak to sit but she stood, occasionally letting out a frustrated pace up and down. "So Akuma told you about your... condition." Jak looked at him. Her face dropped and she felt as if her heart had fallen into her stomach. It was true.

"So, I do have demon's blood; how? Why? How did—" Hasashi held his hand up to stop her. He took her hand and guided her to sit at the end of the bed.

"I cannot tell you how you have this, or why it was given to you. I had my suspicions after Kukiro informed me of your encounter but his visit tonight confirms it. I am sorry I didn't tell you; I did not want to worry you if it turned out to be incorrect." Jak, still feeling broken about hearing this, understood why he didn't say anything. She couldn't look him in the eye; she felt like a monster. Takeda leaned against an empty bed that he was next to in disbelief. He had never heard about this being a thing. He leaned back in to listen to the conversation.

"So, what does this mean for me?" Jak asked. Hasashi sat up.

"Well, it doesn't have to mean anything. Demon's blood in humans tends to remain dormant. However, it can also bring on certain abilities." Jak looked up, intrigued.

"What do you mean, abilities?" Hasashi had a worried look on his face.

"Well, it would be similar to that of Akuma's, possibly other abilities yet to be discovered."

Jak lit up as if she had an idea. "Well, can you train me to use these abilities? It might help us be rid of Akuma!" Hasashi turned away.

"No, it is far too dangerous; we do not know what it could do to you mentally and physically." Jak was ready to protest but Hasashi held up his hand to stop her. "That is the final word on this matter, now please, I think we both need rest; return to your quarters." Takeda quickly slithered out of the room and hurried back to the living quarters to avoid being caught. As he lay there thinking about what he heard, he believed Jak was right. If there is a chance it could work, they should be taking the risk.

He heard Jak coming and quickly rolled over, pretending to be asleep. Jak entered the bedroom quietly so as not to disturb the others, she lay down but could not sleep; her mind was racing about all that happened this evening. She'd decided, regardless of what Hasashi said, she was going to learn about these abilities to help defend her friends; even if it meant risking her life.

Chapter 7

The next morning, Zeke and Toshi took responsibility for overseeing the repairs and fortification, Kukiro was supervising the security of the building, maintaining communication between guards, rotating shifts, training etc. and Triss returned to the medical ward again. Jak entered the library / record room of the Order to look for anything that might help her train in these 'abilities', to help her fight Akuma. She looked in the archives of battles and demons, anything that might describe the abilities they used. She saw a book that was quite old on the top shelf. She stretched and was barely touching it with the tip of her fingers. "You aren't going to find what you are looking for here."

She almost lost her balance and fell after being startled. It was Takeda. She frowned. "Did you follow me?" Takeda nodded. "Besides how do you know what I am looking for?" Takeda walked up to her and looked her dead in the eyes.

"I know." Jak felt a lump in her throat; how could he know? He must be bluffing, she thought to herself.

"Know what?" she said, trying to play it off. Takeda sighed.

"The blood, I know. I followed you last night to Hasashi

and heard your conversation." She felt ugly, pre-judging what he thought about it before knowing. He knows I'm a freak and a monster. She held her head down for a moment, then her head shot up.

"Well, I am going to learn these abilities; neither you nor Grandmaster Hasashi can stop me." Takeda took her hand.

"I am not here to stop you, I am here to help you." Her ears pricked up; she was almost in disbelief.

"Are you sure? Won't you get in trouble?" she asked. Takeda shook his head.

"This is more important. Besides if you were to have these abilities, it makes more sense to know how to control them rather than end up spontaneously using them." She nodded in agreement.

"So where will we find what we need?" Takeda led her to the Grandmaster's temple, to an Oni mask on the wall. He lifted up the mask to reveal a hole. He stuck his arm in, fiddling around. Suddenly, there was a click and the sound of movement in the Grandmaster's chambers. As they entered, they saw a shelf had moved revealing a secret library. Jak looked around in awe at all these ancient scrolls and tomes, all perfectly preserved. Her eyes centred on one that was on a podium. It had been chained and padlocked shut.

"I am going to go out on a limb and say it's the padlocked one?" Jak queried. Takeda simply nodded and took the book. He wrapped up the book in a cloth and placed it in his satchel. They immediately left the room and Jak headed down the stairs of the temple. Takeda closed up the hidden door and replaced the Oni mask, not leaving evidence of their theft. As Takeda caught up, Jak turned and asked, "Where do we go?" Takeda hadn't thought that far. With the temple on high alert guards are almost everywhere; there wasn't a place of privacy.

"We go offsite, into the forest away from the temple and civilisation. Until we know the extent of these abilities, we should avoid any potential casualties." They both agreed and headed to the main gate.

As they reached the main gate and were about to leave, they were stopped by Kukiro. "Where are you two off to? You know the rules, no one is not allowed to leave unless it's for supplies." Jak was trying to think of an excuse but Takeda had already stepped forward.

"I am taking Jak to go to train. As Akuma took an interest to her, I think it is best she be ready to defend herself." Kukiro looked suspicious.

"Why not use the training facilities here?" she questioned, trying to figure out what they are hiding. Again, Takeda on point said, "Safety. It is very crowded and as she has never done anything like this before, I thought it would be wise."

Kukiro, still sure they were hiding something, reluctantly allowed them to go. "All right but be back soon. Grandmaster Hasashi is due to return to his position this evening and he wants to have a meeting with all of us." They nodded and left the grounds. They walked for about thirty minutes east, deeper into the woods. It was so peaceful and secluded; the perfect place to train. Takeda started getting to work at picking the lock on the book.

"So, how did you know about the book? Also, what is in it that makes this a useful one?" Jak asked inquisitively. Takeda, still fiddling with the lock responded.

"I overheard a meeting the Grandmaster had when my father was made the one to take the position. The book is a training manual written one hundred and fifty years ago by the

Grandmaster of then, regarding children with demon blood. Got it!" The lock clicked, releasing the book from its chains which piled on the floor. "Back then he had the demon initiative. He chose an elite team to ingest demon blood to have it as a part of them. Apparently, they made a deal with a demon. In exchange for absolution, he trained them in the ways of the demon; that training was documented in this book."

"So, what happened to the team? And the initiative? Why is it hushed out of existence?" Jak asked, trying to gauge an idea of the risk.

"Well, we can't be too sure, due to the secrecy, but rumours were the team got drunk with power, they started incurring a lot more civilian casualties on missions. When they were told they were to be confined to the temple, they went on a rampage and had to be hunted down. When it came to it, they couldn't kill their brothers and sisters, so the team were subdued and imprisoned. Those tombs? That was the burial place after they passed. After that, the practice was banned and the secrets lost to time, apart from this book."

Jak was concerned. What if she too lost control and ended up hurting others? Just as she was having doubts, she remembered why she was doing this. She knuckled down to focus on the task at hand. "Okay, so what is the first lesson teacher?" Takeda was scanning through the manual.

"So, the first lesson is being able to channel the demon blood. When you are able to do so your eyes will turn black. It says here to do this you need to focus on anger, sadness and hatred to bring it forward. It says you will need to maintain it for around sixty to one hundred and twenty seconds for it to stick. Once you have done it for the first time it should be easier and easier to do. So, get angry."

Takeda was perched on a stump, keeping some distance as this was unchartered territory for both of them. Jak sat there, tensing every muscle, digging deep, focusing on Akuma and everything he'd said, trying to get angry, upset' anything that could trigger this demon blood inside her. She could feel something faint but not enough to trigger it fully. "Dig deeper!" Takeda yelled, trying to push her. She kept digging. She thought about the attack on the temple, the pain around her, the hurt on Takeda and Kukiro's face. Again, a faint stirring. While it was a stronger feeling than before, it wasn't enough. Takeda could see she was not going hard enough, then it hit him, maybe he could push her another way. "Keep pushing. Remember, if you fail, you are signing their lives away, you will be killing your friends." The feeling was bubbling in her more, tears rolling down her face. She was imagining her friends lying in front of her, bloody, beaten, dead. "All of them will be killed if you fail, Jak. Me." 'No,' she thought to herself.

"Zeke."

'No.'

"Triss."

'No.'

"Kukiro."

'NO.'

"Toshi."

'NO, NO, NO!' All of a sudden, she looked up and started screaming at the top of her lungs, wind was encircling her like an aura, leaves being caught in the vortex, her hair standing upright. Takeda was knocked by the initial force but as he rose, he was both amazed and horrified at what he was looking at.

She had done it. She finally stopped screaming and looked at Takeda. She was angry, full of hate, her emerald eyes now pitch black, her tears still streaming had transformed to black. She was breathing heavily. "Okay, you need to hold it Jak. If you can hear me, you hold onto that feeling, stay in control."

She was focusing all her energy to hold the state, she could feel the weight pushing down on her. The image burned into her brain, of her friends and loved ones, dead. Just as she thought that was enough, Akuma appeared in her thoughts hovering over her friends, holding Takeda by the neck who was beaten and unconscious. He was laughing, the anger and hatred was getting stronger. She was paralysed, she wanted to move towards Akuma but couldn't do anything. "Looks like you failed, such a shame," Akuma hissed in his raspy voice. He then turned to the Grandmaster and with a squeeze, he snapped Takeda's neck.

"NO." Jak released another huge scream. The force of the wind pushed Takeda to the ground again, however this time, she screamed forward. The force caused a tree to be ripped from the ground and sent into the trees behind. The weight became more tiresome but Jak stilled pushed through; her hatred for the demon being her driving force. Takeda, struggled to get to his feet, this had gone on for far too long. He needed to snap her out of it.

"Jak! You can let go now, that's enough!" She turned to him, her eyes still black as night, her nose started bleeding.

"It isn't over 'til he is dead!" Her voice had changed, almost like her and Akuma were speaking at the same time.

Takeda, trying to think what he could do to bring her back, got ready to draw his sword as a precaution. The standoff was brief. As Jak was ready to launch her attack on Takeda, she collapsed unconscious onto the ground. Takeda rushed to her aid and he checked to see if she was still breathing. He leant in and felt the faintest of breaths on his ear. He lifted her head up and held her in his arms, rocking her, trying to get some form of reaction. "Wake up Jak, please wake up." She started coughing and gasping for air, the blood from her nose had fallen onto her lips. She could smell the copper of it and the taste; she started wiping it away. Trying to get her bearings, she stood up and almost collapsed again from light-headedness. She maintained her balance thanks to Takeda supporting her.

"I am so sorry Tak, I lost control." Takeda just embraced her and held her tightly.

"Don't worry about it, I am just glad you are okay. Now are you sure you want to keep doing this?" Jak was still trying to catch her breath.

"Yes, we need to. I can harness it, I just need to stay in control but first let's take a little break." They both agreed and sat next to each other. Takeda pulled out two bottles of water and some rice dishes to eat. They sat and relaxed and regain their strength.

About an hour had passed. Jak tried to stand up but didn't have the energy still. "Let's just call it for the day. We can try again tomorrow," Takeda said, helping her to her feet and supporting her as they headed back. "We also may want to pick a closer spot so we don't have to walk as far in this state," he added, both having a chuckle. As they entered the temple grounds, Kukiro dragged them to one side. "Temple, now," she barked at them; she was not very happy. They both looked at each other nervously.

As they arrived, they were dragged to the Grandmaster's

quarters where Kukiro shut the doors and turned back to them. "You two need to explain what happened out there this instant," she demanded. Kukiro had never been so furious before. "I heard the screams, I immediately came out to find you guys, I heard a tree go down unnaturally."

They hung their heads in shame. They filled her in about the demon blood and that they were trying to unlock Jak's abilities.

"You shouldn't be doing this. It's putting yourself and everyone here at risk. I need to tell the Grandmaster about this." Jak stepped forward.

"You can't! This needs to happen. It is dangerous, I am well aware of the risks involved, it is why we are far away from the temple grounds and from civilians. I am going to continue with this regardless, you can't stop me."

Kukiro sighed. "I am sorry, it is for your own good." She began to leave but Takeda grabbed her.

"Please wait! This is a way to prevent any needless bloodshed by fighting Akuma; think of all the lives we can save if we do this. Having this power is a risk, yes but the benefit will outweigh that. Look at the lives lost and the people injured from that attack. That was just a taste of his power, if we go to fight him, he will kill too many for the Order to recover. What if he kills Father, what then?"

Kukiro didn't move, she just thought back to the devastation Akuma left last time. The damage from a full attack could be irreversible, maybe they were right. "Fine, I will keep your secret but you make sure you keep it in check and if you lose control, Tak will not hesitate to end you there and then." Takeda felt unsure about that but to keep the training going, he agreed, Jak also agreed with those terms. If she were to lose control, she would hope that he would end her life; she couldn't bare living if she were to hurt someone she cared about.

"So it is agreed then. Jak please leave us, I need to speak to Takeda alone." Jak almost ran for the door, she could feel the tension in the room and was more than happy to leave. As she shut the door on them, Kukiro turned to Takeda and struck him across his left cheek. "Don't ever lie to me again, especially over something as serious as this. You could've been hurt, you could have been killed! Then how would I explain that to everyone?" Takeda looking down at his feet, holding his cheek which was throbbing from the hit.

"I wanted to tell you but the less this is common knowledge the better. Look at how you originally reacted? It was too risky," he replied.

"I need to know you will be able to handle it if you needed to, killing Jak. I know you have feelings for her, it's obvious but remember, the good of the Order and the world is a priority."

Takeda's right side went bright red to match the mark Kukiro had left, embarrassed he was being called out on his feelings. "I know, but I am prepared." Kukiro looked him up and down then left at a brisk pace, Takeda shortly followed still clutching his cheek. As he emerged, he saw Jak sitting on the top step waiting for him. He proceeded to sit next to her on the step.

"Wow, she really was pissed off," she exclaimed, examining Takeda's cheek.

"Yeah, next time let's include her in our secrets." They both shared a laugh; it was those little moments they would miss, if things were to go wrong.

"So what did she want to speak to you about?" she asked. Takeda wondered whether or not he should be honest with her. "It was about me wasn't it?" Jak added. Takeda, snapping back, realising he didn't answer, decided to go for it.

"Yeah, she wanted to make sure I would be able to go through with... you know, if it came to it." There was a brief silence. Neither of them were sure, what they should say.

"Would you?" Jak asked. "Would you be able to kill me?" Takeda was stunned by this.

"It won't come to that," he reassured.

"Promise me, Tak. If I lose control you don't hesitate to kill me." Another long pause hung in the air. He eventually took her hand and looked at her in the eye.

"I promise."

Chapter 8

As the day drew to a close, the group headed to the Grandmaster's temple to meet with Hasashi. The sky was a deep, reddish purple as the sun faded and the moon rose. The group were nattering between themselves, wondering what it was about but Jak and Takeda were worried he had somehow found they were training. Jak was more worried if he was going to tell Zeke, Triss and Toshi about the demon blood running through her veins. She feared what they would think, how they would react, would they treat her like the monster she felt she was?

As they entered the temple, the Grandmaster was sitting at the same table as when Jak had first met him. He still had some faint bruising from his injuries but he was as composed and strong as ever. They all sat around the table and waited for the Grandmaster to address them. He looked around at them all and smiled. Hasashi had felt so grateful to everyone for their support and strength to maintain the Fallen Lotus in his absence. "First of all, I want to thank all of you. Takeda and Kukiro, you both stood up and showed your leadership, proving you are both worthy successors. Jak, Zeke, Triss and Toshi, you all proved your compassion and love, without any coercing you all helped restore this Order. For that I hope you can accept my small token of gratitude." Hasashi looked towards the gate and clapped his hands. Four women came through carrying boxes, one was placed in front of each of them. They opened them to find robes and gi, stylised to that of the Fallen Lotus.

"I believe they have earned their place among the Fallen Lotus but I cannot alone make this decision. Kukiro, Takeda, do you agree?" They both looked at each other only for a second, then returned their eyes to Hasashi and in unison nodded to confirm their agreement. "Excellent, so it is settled, you four are now members of the Fallen Lotus." They looked at each other all smiling in excitement. Jak's smile quickly faded and turned into a concerned look.

"Grandmaster Hasashi, I am going to assume this wasn't the only reason you summoned us?" His smile left him as he let out a big sigh.

"You are right Jak, I brought you all here to discuss our next steps for dealing with Akuma."

The happy demeanour of everyone shifted to a serious one after he spoke that name. Jak started trembling. Takeda took her hand to calm her down; the last thing they needed would be for her to trigger the blood right there and then. "Those weapons you collected from the tombs are special. They are for slaying demons, erasing them from existence. You will train with them, learn how to use them effectively and efficiently. Takeda, go to the blacksmith, collect the parcel, that will be your weapon." He seemed confused but then he remembered the special instructions he'd dropped off to the blacksmith before the attack.

"I have reason to believe he will strike again soon so you

will need to be prepared. Go and enjoy this evening. Tomorrow you will begin your training." They all stood up and turned to leave. "Jak, Takeda, may I speak with you two alone?" They both looked at each other with the same thought: He Knows.

As the others left, Hasashi signalled the guards to close the large doors and as they shut, Hasashi just looked at them both. A minute had passed but to Takeda and Jak, it felt like an hour. Finally, Hasashi spoke. "So, is there anything you two want to tell me?" Jak was worried. Either he knows or he is trying to get them to reveal it on their own; the pressure was getting too much.

"It was my idea, Father!" Jak turned to Takeda in disbelief, what was he doing? "Jak wanted to learn but I put everything into place. I took the book, I took her to train, I read the texts. It is my burden to bear." Hasashi just smiled at him.

"I am not a fool Takeda. While I am sure you did do a lot of those things you wouldn't have been able to without Jak."

Jak chimed in. "Hang on, how did you find out? Did Kukiro tell you?" Jak was puzzled considering the Grandmaster he was on bed rest when they were training.

"Well, after our conversation last night I thought about what you said, so I left bed rest early to go to get the book. When I found it missing and that you two were gone, I put things together. Nothing gets passed me," he said, with a cheeky little smile afterwards. Jak, still confused, had one more question.

"Why were you getting the book? After our conversation I would've assumed you'd be against it. Why are you not angry that we went against what you wanted?"

Hasashi just looked at her. "After that conversation, you would have been right. My plan originally was to burn the book to prevent this. But then I realised I was making a decision which wasn't mine to make. It is your life; it is yours to do with as you wish. If this is what you truly want to do, I will not stop you. I do ask though, that you know the risks that are involved."

Takeda took his hand. "She knows father, I told her about the origins of the book. She still wishes to go ahead, she has a lot of potential, she managed to do in one session what the others took weeks to achieve; she can handle it." He turned to Jak who smiled back. She felt warmth coming from the belief Takeda had in her. Hasashi looked at them both.

"Very well, you two will conduct your training off grounds, split weapon and 'special' training and remember Jak…" He leaned in towards her. "Remember who you are and what you are fighting for." Jak knew what he meant by that. It is easy to get lost in the power of the blood; it is overwhelming. She nodded firmly and left with Takeda.

"Thank you Tak," Jak said to him as they were walking down the steps.

"For what?" he replied. She took his hand and they stopped, looking into each other's eyes.

"For believing in me, for not treating me like a freak, for being there for me. You make me feel like, well, me." She gave him a hug, she then leaned back. Still in each other's embrace, eyes locked, Takeda took the chance and leaned in. Jak reciprocated, both their hearts racing as their lips met under the stars of the night sky, the luminescent glow of the moon shining down on them. In that moment, everything disappeared: there was no Akuma, no Fallen Lotus, it was only them, nothing else mattered. Time was non-existent, their surroundings a blur.

"Get a room you two!" They both pulled away and turned to the bottom of the staircase. It was Zeke, Triss, Toshi and Kukiro. Triss smacked Zeke round the head.

"You idiot! Why did you ruin the moment!" As they reached the bottom of the stairs, Toshi and Kukiro approached.

"Sorry, Zeke insisted we waited so we can start the celebrations together and it seems we have another thing to celebrate!" Toshi exclaimed. He was so happy for Jak and gave her a massive hug. Kukiro was more reserved but couldn't help but smile for them, even if she still had reservations as to whether Takeda would be able to kill her if she lost control. Kukiro decided not to bring it up. Everyone would need this night to relax. What followed would be a horrendous challenge which would push them to their limits.

The group sat in the dining quarters, eating, drinking and laughing. It wasn't just them either, others joined in, celebrating their new brothers and sisters, as well as the coupling of Takeda and Jak. Jak felt slightly awkward as it was still all new and people kept going on about the future. It started freaking her out but Takeda would grab her hand, look her in the eyes and smile and all of her worries and panic would melt away. She couldn't explain it but there was something about him that made her feel so comfortable and confident that she could face anything, even the challenges ahead.

As the night progressed, people kept dropping out, first Toshi and Kukiro went to bed, followed shortly by Triss and Zeke. Eventually the dining area was empty apart from Takeda and Jak. They were still talking and laughing, not even realising they were alone until they got up to go for a walk. They left the grounds and went to the woods, beams of moonlight breaking through the branches, dotting the pathway.

"So, can we talk about the kiss?" Takeda asked. Jak didn't know what to say. "I have feelings for you Jak and I really think this can go somewhere. How do you feel about it? What do you think?" Jak started panicking again, she hadn't been very good at showing emotions like this before.

"I don't know Tak, it would be difficult. After all I have demon blood and it's not just that, I am not an easy person. I do have feelings for you but wouldn't it be easier for you to be with someone else?" Takeda stopped, he took her hand and pulled her in close.

"I don't care about the demon blood or if our relationship will be easy. The hardest things are usually worth fighting for. I don't want to be with anyone else, I want to be with you from now until the end of time. Being with you is worth any hardships and challenges we will face, because we will be facing them together." He then pulled her in and kissed her with a fiery passion. Jak wanted to resist but fell into it, that same feeling from the first kiss flowing through her. She wanted this too, no matter how hard she tried to deny it; her heart wanted him.

In the heat of the moment, they collapsed to the ground not retracting from each other for a second. No sounds were to be heard apart from the rustling of leaving and moans of passion as they made love right there and then. After, they just laid there. A little clearing in the trees meant they could look up at the night sky whilst in their warm embrace. Jak still felt as if she shouldn't go down this path but she didn't want to fight what her heart wanted. Instead, she was in the moment, not thinking about the future or about what could happen. She was just there and there was no place she would rather be. An hour or two passed before they decided to return to the Fallen Lotus grounds and go to bed; they would need some rest for the following morning's training.

The mood in the morning, in contrast to the previous evening, was very tense. Everyone knew what they were training for, what they had to do and they were all focused on the task at hand. Jak, Triss, Zeke and Toshi were all dressed in their new gear determined, focused and ready for the day ahead of them. As they reached the end of the courtyard near the gate, Jak and Takeda headed towards the main gate whereas the others split off to the training grounds. Toshi was the first to notice. "Hey where are you guys going? Are you not training?" he asked, puzzled.

Jak and Takeda stopped and hesitated, trying to think of a reason as to why they needed to train separately. Before they could come up with a response, Grandmaster Hasashi interrupted them. "It is under my request. Takeda you left your package at the blacksmith." Takeda completely forgot about collecting it before heading out. Hasashi handed him the long box for which Takeda bowed. Hasashi dipped his head in recognition then turned to Toshi. "His new weapon requires more room, so he is leaving the grounds to train, Jak is going as Takeda is her instructor."

Toshi still didn't seem to understand but didn't want to question the Grandmaster. Zeke chimed up, "Don't you two have too much fun," jokingly, followed by a smack round the head from Triss.

"Jackass," she muttered under her breath. Both Takeda and Jak went bright red. Hasashi looked at them and raised an eyebrow. Kukiro jumped in.

"You two, go and begin your training, you three follow

me." Jak and Takeda almost ran out of the gates in a hurry to escape that situation. Once they were clear, they both looked at each other and started laughing; neither of them knew why, it just happened.

They reached the same place where they were training last time. Jak looked over at the tree she had taken down, still in awe that she was the cause of that but also slightly fearful. If that was just the start of her power, imagine the damage she could cause at her full potential. No, Jak reminded herself, she was in control and she was going to stay that way. As she was mentally readying herself to activate the blood again, Takeda at the collapsed tree placed his parcel on top and began to open it up. Inside were two swords. However, they were long, thin and flat on the top; they seemed more like bladed rods. Takeda removed them from the box, puzzled by their design and noticed when looking up and down, there were inlays on each blade.

As he rotated one of them to see if the inlays went all the way round, he squeezed the handle. All of a sudden, the blade collapsed but was not broken as Takeda feared when it happened. The blades were designed for being used as swords but they were also made to fully function as razor whips. He looked at the other blade in his hand and squeezed the handle causing it to collapse. His look of amazing was comparable to that of a child at Christmas. He started waving them round elegantly as if they were just extensions of his arms and he was performing a dance. They felt good to Takeda: light, balanced, and very sharp. He wrapped one round a branch of a tree and pulled. The branch didn't simply break, it was cut and it was a clean cut too; like a knife through butter.

"Those are pretty cool!" Jak chimed in. Takeda nearly

stumbled, he forgot he wasn't alone for a second.

"I know, I love them." He paused for a second, looking up and down the handles. "I just need to figure out how to put them back." That's when he remembered the flattened tips. He held the whip flat and started pushing against the ground. Slowly the whip started retracting and the blade segments interlocking. As they all finished locking together there was a satisfying click and it was once again a sword.

Takeda placed them back into the box for now as they wanted to focus on the blood training first. "Right Jak, let us begin. When you are ready, activate the blood. It should be easier this time." He hadn't looked back, as he was looking over the blades.

"Umm Tak?" Still not taking his eyes off the blades as he was looking for something, he responded.

"Remember, think of what made you angry." That's when he found it: an inscription on the tip of the blades.

"Tak!" He stopped looking and turned around.

"What is wrong Jak?" As he turned, he noticed it too. Her eyes were black and the wind-like aura was calm, albeit moving her hair. She had activated it and it seemed to be sustaining. As he stood and stared on, she just turned to him and with a slightly sadistic smile uttered, "I think I am ready."

Chapter 9

A week had passed since the group started their vigorous training to prepare for the battle ahead. Everyone was feeling confident in their new found abilities, apart from Jak. She felt a lot more in control of her demon powers but she felt as though Takeda was withholding information from her. As Takeda was practicing with his whip blades, she was looking through the book and she found it. By looking at the image paired with the text in the book, she saw that it depicted a human with the power, dragging a demon down to hell, chains reaching up and grabbing them both.

"Tak, what is this?" She asked, wanting to know more. He stopped waving his whips, transformed them back into the blade forms and sheathed them. As he looked over and saw the page Jak had the book open on, he tried to close it.

"It is nothing, don't worry." Jak had kept her thumb on the page so immediately flipped it back open.

"Tak, you know I am not going to drop it, just tell me."

He sighed. "Fine but that is all that is going to happen with this, okay? I don't want to hear about it anymore." She nodded as he sat down and took the book. "It is called the Saigo no nozomi, or last hope. A person imbued with these powers essentially boils over and lets the blood consume them. In a last ditched effort, they charge the demon and drag them down to hell." Jak looked at it as he was pointing to the image, showing the chains reaching up for the demon.

"So why haven't you shown me this? This could end the fight in an instant! No needless bloodshed!" Jak stood up, feeling frustrated at him for not telling her about this. Tak simply reached for her hand and brought her back down next to him.

"Because it is not worth it Jak. The cost is too great; look." He tapped on the book showing chains shooting up to the fighter. "Yes, the demon gets sent back to hell but the person who sends him gets trapped there as well."

Jak felt a sudden chill roll down her spine. Being trapped in hell must be a terrible fate. She turned and saw the look on Takeda's face; a look of fear. She wrapped her arms around him from the side and kissed his cheek. "Don't worry Tak, I won't use it." He turned to her.

"Do you promise me?" She smiled.

"I promise." They kissed and embraced each other in a comforting hug. Unfortunately, Takeda didn't know that she was lying. She knew she would have to read and learn this technique as a last resort. She hated lying to him but she thought it would be for the best, so as Takeda continued his training, she continued studying the page.

As they both returned to the temple grounds the other four approached them. Kukiro in front greeted them first. "Welcome back, I trust training went well?" They nodded in agreement. "Good, we have been summoned by the Grandmaster, he wants us all to see him immediately." They all headed to the Grandmaster's chambers but were cut off by a guard.

"Kukiro, you and the rest need to go to the medical wing, you will find the Grandmaster there." They all looked confused and worried as to why they needed to head there. Their pace quickened as they hurried to assess the situation.

When they arrived, they saw the Grandmaster standing next to a bed looking over an injured, bloody man, surrounded by doctors attending to his wounds. Hasashi turned and saw the group. He said goodbye to the man and headed to them, looking furious. "Damn that Akuma," he muttered under his breath, as he stormed out of there. Everyone caught up and followed him.

"Grandmaster Hasashi, what happened? Who was that man?" Zeke asked. Hasashi turned around.

"Not here, I don't want to cause a panic, please follow me." They retreated to the Grandmaster's quarters and the guards closed the doors. "To answer your questions Zeke, that man was the leader of a scout party I commissioned to keep tabs on Akuma, whilst you were training. He was the only one to make it back; Akuma picked them apart like they were nothing. I will spare you the details." They all looked at each other sceptically. "Kukiro, Takeda, do you think your team is ready?" Takeda and Kukiro looked at each other.

"Ready for what Grandmaster? Surely you can't expect them to fight Akuma?" Kukiro exclaimed. As confident as the group were, it had only been a week's worth of training; they needed more time.

"We have no choice. We need to strike him tonight."

Takeda was hoping with all his heart that his father was just telling a joke that was in bad taste but he could see that he was serious. "What did the scout tell you father?" fearing the answer. "We know where Akuma is and what he is doing. He is planning to open a gate to hell and release every demon onto earth. He will be planning to open it at Komayama Park in Kanagawa."

They all looked at each other again. It all still felt surreal to them but also it felt as if it was par for the course. Each one began to realise that what they were going to face, where they were going, could very well be the last place they see. Kukiro banged on the table. "We can't!" Everyone was staring at her. "Grandmaster I get the urgency but we are not ready; he will tear us apart." Hasashi looked at Kukiro. She was right but he didn't see a lot of options, except one.

"I was hoping we could avoid this, but there is only one other option." He turned to Jak. "Do you think you are ready?" Jak looked at him hesitantly.

"Umm, maybe? I am not sure, I think I might be able to do it."

Triss, Toshi and Zeke, all unaware of Jak's power, were confused. "Grandmaster Hasashi, with all due respect to both you and Jak, why would she be ready and us not? She has had the same training as us," Toshi asked. Hasashi continued to look at Jak. She looked down, then back to Hasashi and nodded.

"Toshi, Zeke, Triss, there is something you have not been told at the respect of Jak's wishes. Only Takeda, Kukiro and myself are informed of her situation. She has undergone different training off grounds so as not to alert the others. Jak would you like to demonstrate?" They all turned to Jak who sheepishly stood up and took a few paces away from them.

She took a deep breath and closed her eyes. She opened them forcefully to reveal pure, black pits, the energy surrounding her flowing calmly. The three could not believe what they were seeing; they weren't even sure *what* they were seeing. Takeda went over to Jak and took her hand. She closed her eyes and just like that, the aura faded. As she opened her eyes, they had returned to their usual emerald selves. "What was that?" Triss asked, the other two still gobsmacked.

"That Triss, was demon blood, or what controlling it can do." Takeda and Jak sat back down, to which Takeda interjected.

"It doesn't matter, she isn't ready. Let me and Kukiro go; we are the most adept. Don't let them go, they are not ready." Hasashi smacked his fist against the table.

"Enough! You all will go, you and Kukiro, as formidable as you may be, will not be enough, you all need each other."

Jak waved her hands in front of everyone, gesturing for them to calm down. "We will all go. We may not have the strength for a full-frontal assault but I have a plan." About two hours had passed. They kept going over the plan, making sure everyone knew their part, where they needed to position themselves and when they needed to strike. It got to mid-afternoon before they were ready to set off. Mentally preparing themselves, they all got in the truck and set off for the fight.

They pulled up about half a mile away from the park. It was night-time, the skies were clear and the moon was out. The team all geared up and prepared for the fight of their lives. After they were ready, they all stood in a circle. Zeke was the first to speak. "I know this isn't what we all want to think about but I want you all to know, in case we don't make it back, you are the best friends a guy could ask for; I am glad I have you all by my side." They all smiled as they were all thinking it too; they all have a bond and are glad they are all together for this. They all closed in, had a group hug and some tears were shed.

"Right guys," Jak said, pulling away and wiping a tear from her eyes. "I know it is going to be hard. I will go on ahead, you all follow me five minutes after and get into position as we discussed."

The group all nodded, then Jak made her way, focused and ready to take on the beast that is Akuma. She reached a clearing and saw a figure just standing there, looking into the sky, directly at the moon. She tried to sneak up and close the gap but before she could, the figure spoke. "It's a beautiful night tonight, it is a shame you won't see another one like it Jak." The figure turned around, revealing those piercing, white eyes that Jak knew all too well; the ones from her nightmares. It was Akuma.

"The only one not leaving here tonight is you, Akuma. It was my fault you are here; I am going to correct my mistake." Fear gripped her body but she knuckled down and forced herself to move forward. Akuma, his hands behind his back, approached relaxed and laughing.

"And I thought we had a bond. After all, it was I who revealed to you your true self. You seem pretty confident. Will you make it worth my while?"

They both stopped in their tracks, a foot in between them. "You are too late Jak, I have already set up for the gate to be opened. At midnight, all of hell will empty and the takeover of earth will begin." Jak just stood there unphased, much to the confusion of Akuma.

"Well then I guess I will have to end this quickly." Jak clenched her fists, took a deep breath then transformed, her aura pulsating, eyes black and focused on Akuma with a sadistic smile across her face. Akuma was taken aback by this, but then started laughing.

"So, you actually did it willingly! Wow I thought you were purer than that! I guess the old man was desperate! But you are a fool if you think you can take me on."

Before Akuma could do anything however, Jak raised her hands and clenched them into fists. Akuma tried moving but was frozen still. "Very clever Jak but now you are stuck like this. You shouldn't have come alone." Jak's nose started bleeding, the strain of holding someone of his power was taking its toll but she refused to show it; she simply smiled.

"Who said I was alone?" Akuma looked confused then felt it, the others in the woods; he had let his guard down. His eyes darted around as five figures emerged from the tree lines behind Jak.

In a panic, Akuma started struggling, trying to free himself from Jak's grasp but she was refusing to let go. "Now!" Kukiro yelled out. Triss strung her bow and fired two arrows, hitting him in his eyes. Akuma let out a roar in pain. Jak could feel her grip weakening fast but just focused on Akuma again. Black lines had started appearing on her face as if shooting out from her eyes, her grip tightened. Takeda approached, turning his blades into whips. He was spinning them faster and faster until they were a blur. Using the momentum, he sliced off both of Akuma's arms at the shoulders. Akuma dropped to his knees, letting out another chilling roar in the process. Toshi circled round behind the demon and charged at him with all his might. He drove the shield into Akuma's back, causing him to go face first into the ground. Almost as soon as the dirt settled, Kukiro was in the air and dropped down, stabbing Akuma through the back and pinning him down to the ground.

"Zeke now!" she yelled. Zeke began to charge. Jak could feel something was wrong; Akuma was no longer resisting. At first, she thought he had been hurt so much, he didn't have the energy but she could feel something was wrong. She focused on him. The darkness made it hard to make out what was happening but as she focused, she saw it, a smile and a bright, piercing, white eye. He wasn't resisting because he was focusing on recuperating.

"Everyone! Get back!" Jak yelled but it was too late as Zeke arrived, his axe over his head ready to strike,

Akuma let out an ear-piercing roar and exerted a massive force, launching everyone. Toshi stayed on his feet as his shield took the brunt of the force. He managed to catch Kukiro. Zeke got sent flying past Jak and landed next to Triss, who quickly dropped her bow to check on him. Takeda got knocked down but quickly got back up and was ready to strike again. Jak withstood the blast but dropped to her knees. Holding Akuma for as long as she did, had drained her and she needed to catch her breath.

Akuma stood up. He had fully restored himself as if they hadn't even touched him. "That was very sneaky Jak, kudos to everyone, you did well. But not good enough. Now you will pay." Akuma picked up Kukiro's sword and began to approach Jak. Takeda stepped in front of Jak. With his whips returned to swords he prepared himself for battle.

"As long as I live you will not touch her!" he declared. Akuma just smirked.

"No problem." Takeda charged in head first ready to fight. He was swinging rapidly but no matter what angle or how fast he attacked, Akuma easily blocked and dodged the attacks.

Akuma went on the offensive. He was so fast; Takeda could barely keep up with his strikes. He kept getting pushed back by the demon until he was mere feet away from the tree line. Akuma then launched a fireball from his breath. Takeda tried to dodge but got clipped on his shoulder; the fireball splintered off into the woodland which caught fire. Takeda lay on the ground clutching his shoulder in agony, the smell of smouldering flesh surrounding him.

"You fought well but you were no match for me. But do you know what? I am not going to kill any of you just yet." He started walking to the centre of the clearing. "I want you to witness the beginning of the end. And the end starts now!" As he finished his sentence, he closed his eyes and held his hands, pointing to the ground in front of him. The ground started to shake and the moon was changing from brilliant white to blood red. A dark essence was emerging from Akuma's body and forming a circle on the ground.

Once the circle had completed the ground stopped shaking, little sparks of purple and red electricity started shooting around the circle and then from out of nowhere, a pillar of thick, black smoke shot out of the ground into the sky in a spiral like a tornado. Akuma had done it.

The Gate was open.

Chapter 10

The Gate had been opened, demons were pouring out into the world, the team could do nothing but just stare on in terror of what was awaiting the world. The dark cloud of evil creating a vortex in the sky, the blood red moon, Akuma laughing with triumph and arrogance was a truly horrific sight. "You see? I told you there was nothing you could do. I will be your god!" Akuma yelled out. Feeling the taste of victory gave him such pleasure. Everyone was still on the ground, either in pain or helping their friends. Jak stumbled to her feet and started to let go, her rising anger causing her powers to become unstable. The marks across her eyes were spreading across her entire body, fangs were starting to protrude like that of a vampire, her nails and fingertips turned black and into claws.

"You call yourself a god," she said, breathing heavily, staring Akuma down. Akuma just looked at her, amused at her attempt to challenge him again. She kept stepping towards him, not breaking her pace. "But what is a god, to a non-believer!" She broke into a sprint and lunged at him, taking him by surprise. He dropped to the ground; Jak digging her claws into his chest, letting out a roar similar to Akuma's.

A plume of smoke broke away from the vortex and

sideswiped Jak, knocking her off Akuma. She flipped sideways but landed on her feet. Akuma stood up and started clapping. "Yes Jak! Let go! Become the demon you were meant to be!" Jak was losing herself but still maintaining some form of control, she was aware that he was baiting her. She charged him again. Akuma, ready this time, threw a fireball at her but she dodged it without losing any momentum. She used her power, picked up Kukiro's sword and slashed at him. He managed to dodge the first few swipes but got caught on the arm and nearly lost his balance. Just as Jak seemed to be gaining the upper hand, two more plumes of smoke shot out of the vortex. Two demons started materialising out of the smoke between Akuma and Jak.

They started attacking her, forcing her back. Kukiro got back to her feet. "Toshi, go help Triss with Zeke. I will go to Takeda, we need to help Jak!" They split up. Triss managed to get Zeke propped up against a tree, he was bleeding heavily from his forehead.

"Tosh help me, I need to stop the bleeding!" Triss cried. He sat there and thought about what to do. He tore off some fabric from his trousers and placed it over the wound.

"Keep pressure on it, stay with him; I need to help Jak!" Toshi stood up and headed over to Takeda and Kukiro.

Takeda was sitting up. He was already wrapping up his burns using his sleeves. Toshi slid next to them. "Okay guys, what's the plan?" he asked, eyes darting between both of them. They looked over and saw the other two who were in no condition to fight. They then turned to each other and nodded in agreement.

"You need to take Zeke and Triss back to the truck. We have medical supplies there to patch him up. We will help Jak,"

Kukiro said. Toshi couldn't believe he was being side-lined.

"I can fight! Let me help!" Kukiro brought him in close.

"Please Toshi, I know you can but the best way you can help us is to ensure their safety." He reluctantly agreed. "Please stay alive," he said to her, tearing up. She gave him a kiss.

"I will." Then she and Takeda got up and ran to help Jak.

As Toshi, Triss and Zeke were retreating back to the vehicle, Jak had been pushed back against a tree, the sword had been knocked out of her hand. She was using her power to hold the ravenous demons back when all of a sudden, two whip blades wrapped around their necks. It was Takeda. He pulled back, tightening the grip, eventually decapitating them. Kukiro picked up her sword and both went to check on Jak. "Jak are you okay?" Takeda asked. She pushed away.

"I am fine. Leave." She was losing control; she could feel it. Kukiro pulled him away and put her hand on Jak's shoulder.

"Can you beat him?" Jak was trying to hold back the anger but it was becoming too powerful, the conflict was putting a massive strain on her. She realised what she had to do.

"Yes." She managed to mutter. Kukiro nodded.

"Tak, Jak is going to focus on Akuma, we need to keep the demons off her back." Tak was looking at Jak. He feared he was going to lose her and he would have to take her life. "Tak!" Kukiro yelled. He snapped out of it. He looked at Kukiro. She could sense what was going through his mind just by the look on his face. "Tak, she will be fine, we will save her but right now we need to protect her!" He quickly nodded and prepared to fight.

Jak looked at Akuma, who had a look of fear on his face. "Nowhere to run this time Akuma! Ready to die?" Jak said, antagonising the demon. He didn't take too kindly to the verbal jab and his look of fear quickly descended into anger. He lunged in to attack Jak but she was too quick. She sidestepped and drove her elbow into his spine causing him to yell in pain. She looked over at the base of the vortex. It quivered. "So, to stop the Gate, I have to get rid of you. This will be quick." She proceeded to pick him up and throw him into the tree. He went straight through shattering the trunk, shards of wood flying off in every direction. As Jak continued to assault Akuma, Kukiro and Takeda we dealing with any demons coming to the aid of Akuma.

Another three materialised out of the vortex, one attacking Kukiro and two going after Takeda. He was slower because of his wound but it didn't stop him, he charged them without fear. They savagely clawed at him but were not able to deal any damage. He blocked every attack with fierce precision and quickly dispatched each of them. Kukiro did not struggle either; they were quick to dispatch the demons.

Akuma rose up after being launched across the battlefield once more, more and more frustrated. "NO, NO, NO! YOU ARE NOT SUPPOSED TO BE THIS STRONG! I WILL KILL YOU!" he yelled, his blood boiling. H grabbed her and tossed her into the vortex, sending her spiralling. He jumped in after her. Hurtling through the air, they were both landing strike after strike on each other. Jak slashed across his face, cutting his mask and drawing blood. He jolted back, roaring in agony. However, he started to laugh. Jak paused for a moment before she was grabbed from behind. Demons materialised in the vortex, restricting her movement. "This is where you DIE!" As soon as Akuma finished that sentence, he drove his claws into the side of Jak who cried out in pain. The demons let go. Akuma, claws still inside, pulled her out of the vortex and drove her down to the ground.

Takeda and Kukiro had to dodge out of the way as they came crashing to the ground causing a violent eruption of dirt and dust. As the ground settled and the air cleared, they both looked on in horror as out of the pit created from the impact, only Akuma emerged. "Now I didn't have to kill you two but after what that little bitch just did, I am going to make it slow and painful," he continued, approaching them; his hands dripping with Jaks blood, his face oozing his.

Takeda and Kukiro looked on. They saw Jak was still alive but barely. Takeda immediately jumped in and started attacking, not feeling anything but a burning rage for what Akuma did to Jak. However, he was too hurt and exhausted to gain any advantage. Akuma easily dodged his attacks and quickly launched him backwards, knocking him unconscious.

Kukiro ran to his side and helped him up. She couldn't feel anything. This was it, she wasn't going to see anyone again: Takeda, Hasashi, but most of all, she would miss Toshi. She started to feel regret. "I am sorry Toshi, I am going to miss you," she muttered to herself, as a tear rolled down her cheek. Akuma reached her, bringing her head up with one claw.

"Don't worry dear, you will see him soon. Once I am done here, he is next." He started to laugh maniacally; she couldn't do anything but cry.

"Kukiro!" a weak voice cried out. It was Jak, a furious aura sparking around her, her wounds still bleeding out. She was shuffling forward. "Tell them I love them. Toshi, Zeke, Triss. Tell them I am sorry I couldn't do it any other way." Akuma dropped Kukiro's chin and turned around.

"You are a persistent one, aren't you? You just don't know when to die." He started to move forward but suddenly froze;

he couldn't move at all. Jak was holding him still.

"Kukiro, promise me…" She coughed up blood and spat it to the ground. "Promise me, that you will tell Takeda this too: I love him and I am sorry I had to break my promise." Kukiro was so confused.

"PROMISE ME!" she yelled, her voice becoming more and more demonic, slipping deeper and deeper into madness. Kukiro flinched but nodded. Jak smiled. "Good." She then waved her left hand, launching Kukiro and Takeda through the trees almost all the way back to the car.

Akuma started laughing. "What are you going to do? You couldn't kill me when you weren't beaten, you definitely won't now."

Jak let out a small exhausted chuckle. "I may not be able to kill you," she arrived face to face with him and grabbed him by the neck; Akuma beginning to panic, "but I can take you away from here." Her aura started becoming more and more powerful. She finally, after being in control for as long as she could, let go. She had gone full demon. "Time to say goodbye." As she let out all of her power, the ground beneath them began to drop out, revealing a bottomless pit. Akuma realised what was happening and started to flail about, trying to escape her grasp but to no avail. Out of the darkness of the pit, hooked chains shot up and started to pierce their flesh. Akuma yelling in defeat, Jak letting out a single tear, the last shred of her human; self-managing one last thought before succumbing to the darkness: Goodbye.

They were dragged down into the darkness. Shortly after they disappeared, the pit closed up leaving nothing but cracks forming the circle. With Akuma gone, the Gate closed, the vortex dissipated rapidly revealing a clear night sky, stars were twinkling and the blood red moon returned to its pure luminescence. The hellfire that was burning through the woods had fizzled out. Jak had done it; peace had been restored.

Chapter 11

"Jak!"

Takeda shot up in the back of the truck, dazed and confused. He looked around; everyone was crying. "Guys, what happened?" He looked up. The vortex was no longer there and the moon was brilliantly white again. "She did it? Let's go get her, guys!" He leapt out of the truck, completely ignoring the pain in his shoulder.

"Wait Tak!" Kukiro called out. He stopped and turned to her.

"What are we waiting for? She could be seriously hurt." He just looked at them, confused. He saw they were all crying profusely. "No... sh-she didn't, she wouldn't... she promised me." He ran to the woods, tears rolling down his face. He refused to believe it. He reached the wreckage that was the scene of the battle. He looked around but there were no bodies. Then he saw the cracked circle where the pit opened and he dropped to his knees. "You promised me." The tears wouldn't stop.

Kukiro and the others caught up with him. "Tak." Kukiro touched his shoulder. He leapt up and stood next to the circle; he drew his sword and started stabbing at the ground.

"Bring her back. You bring her back! She doesn't belong there!" Everyone was becoming more emotional, seeing Takeda break down this way.

"Tak, please stop," Kukiro begged. He threw the sword away and started beating the ground.

"Please... bring her back... Jak... you promised me," he muttered to himself, his voice breaking as he broke down. The group all gathered round and sat with him, holding him, trying to console him. They all broke down and cried together. They had lost their friend; someone they had loved.

Three weeks had passed since Jak had sacrificed herself to save her friends and the world. There was a gathering held in the courtyard to honour her sacrifice; to pay tribute to what she did for everyone. Hasashi was the first to speak. "We are gathered to pay tribute to Jak, she gave her life to protect not only us but the whole world, from Akuma. In honour of what she did, we erect this statue of Jak." He signalled for two people to remove a tarp revealing a stone statue of Jak. A bronze plaque was on the base, it read: Jak Wyatt, a friend to all, a true hero of the Fallen Lotus.

Hasashi continued. "Let us not forget her; she gave everything to defend what she loved. We shall all do our best to follow in her footsteps. I now pass you over to Zeke to speak." Zeke stepped forward.

"Unfortunately, I am not the best with words but I can tell you all, Jak was a genuine person. She may have seemed cold at times but once you got to know her, she would open up and show you truly what an amazing person she was..." Triss looked around, she couldn't see Takeda anywhere. She leaned over to Kukiro.

"Where is Tak?" she whispered, trying not to interrupt Zeke.

"In the library. He has been there for three days straight," she replied. Triss looked towards the library, there was no sign of him coming.

"I am going to go get him."

As she entered the library, she could hear a faint rustling of papers in the distance. It must have been him as everyone else was at the service. As she rounded the corner of a bookshelf, she saw him. He was wrapped in a blanket, sitting down, reading through some old scrolls, dirty dishes scattered round him as well as a pillow; although it looked like he hadn't slept in the three weeks since.

"Tak?" No response. "Tak? What are you doing? Why aren't you at the service for Jak?" Still no response. She moved in closer, slowly as if he was a deer and she was trying not to startle him. She accidentally tripped over a dish and Takeda's head shot up, looking at her.

"Triss? When did you get here?" he asked, wild eyed, as if he had just snapped out of a trance.

"I was calling you. Why aren't you with everyone at the service?" He looked back down at the scrolls he was reading.

"She isn't dead," he said. Triss looked confused.

"What do you mean she isn't dead? She is gone Takeda. I know it is hard but if you come to the service-"

"NO," Takeda snapped, cutting Triss off. "I will not give up on her. The book says they get taken to hell with the Oni. I will find a way to bring her back; there has to be something here. There just has to be." He threw the scrolls across the floor in frustration, his head fell into his hands and he began to weep. Triss moved in and put her arm around him, trying to stop from crying as well.

"Tak, I get it, she loved you and you loved her. It is why she did what she did; she did it to save you. She wouldn't want to see you like this, you know that. She would want you to pick yourself up and continue fighting the fight she started. Do it for her Tak."

He looked up at her, tears welling in his eyes. "I don't think I can Triss." She looked back to the exit, then she had an idea.

"Come with me, I want to show you something." He reluctantly followed her to the entrance of the library. As they exited, he needed to shield his eyes from the daylight, he had been in the library for so long. As his vision adjusted, he saw it. A sea of Fallen Lotus paying tribute to Jak. "You see? Look at how many people she saved and look at all of them paying their respects. She touched each and every one of them with her bravery. She would want you to be brave, to save the lives she won't be able to." He was still in awe of the size of the crowd. Triss was right, Takeda thought. He removed his blanket and headed down to join his brothers and sisters in honouring the one he loved.

Triss returned to her place next to Kukiro. "Thank you Triss," Kukiro whispered. Triss nodded and continued to listen to Zeke's words. It was a beautiful day, Takeda began to think to himself; Jak would've loved it.

The next day, the team had a meeting with Hasashi who had an important announcement to make. Takeda was the last one to arrive. "Look who washed!" Zeke shouted. Takeda just smiled and held his hands up.

"I know I haven't been the easiest person to be around since… you know. I just want to thank everyone for their patience with me, your care and support has really got me through." He looked particularly at Triss due to her words at the library. She just smiled back. She was happy to see how was starting to get back on his feet.

"So, does anyone know why we're here?" Toshi asked. Everyone reacted the same, clueless.

"You are here because you chose to be." Everyone turned to see the Grandmaster approaching with a box. "Whether it be Zeke, Triss and Toshi choosing to stay and help or whether it be Kukiro and Takeda, you both were raised here but chose to stay. You have all chosen to stay."

He arrived at the group. They all took a seat around the table and Hasashi placed the box on top. "However, I must ask you all to leave." They all seemed shocked and confused at the request. Kukiro spoke up.

"Grandmaster Hasashi, have we done something wrong?" He smiled.

"No child, you must leave, because this world needs you."

"What do you mean?" Zeke asked. "The Gate was closed right? Akuma is gone." Hasashi waved his hand asking for patience from the group.

"You are correct Zeke," a voice called out. A man in a suit emerged from the shadows. "Akuma is gone and the Gate was closed but the damage remains; thousands of demons were let loose in the time it was open. Without Akuma a lot have gone into hiding, regaining their strength. They are not as nearly as strong as Akuma but if they were to go unchallenged, it could spell disaster." He approached the group. Takeda stood up ready to draw his sword.

"Takeda! Sit down!" Grandmaster shouted, grabbing his hand to prevent him from drawing his blade.

"Father, who is this man?" Grandmaster Hasashi turned to the stranger.

"Please, allow me to introduce myself. My name is Jiryen. I am an ambassador for the GDA: the Global Defence Agency. We are a secret group under the jurisdiction of the UN."

They all seemed sceptical. It was all a little too convenient. "The GDA specialises in dealing with the hellspawn like Akuma. However, our presence must maintain the utmost secrecy which is why I am here. We saw how you handled yourselves with Akuma -" Toshi cut him off.

"Wait, if you saw it, why not help? Why did you not intervene?" Jiryen let out a sigh.

"I wanted to, however the higher-ups prevented it. They wanted to see if you had potential."

"Potential for what?" Kukiro asked. Jiryen held up his hand.

"I understand you all have questions but please let me finish and I will answer them all the best I can after I have said what I need to say. Deal?" The group looked around the table, exchanging glances of distrust about the stranger. However, they all agreed to hear him out. Jiryen smiled. "Excellent! Now to business, the GDA would like to… how to put it… sponsor you, if you will. We will fund you and provide any equipment you may need. In exchange, for us you are to travel the world, hunting these demons that were brought here through the Gate." They all were intrigued by the offer. Jiryen continued. "We will be a silent partner; no one can know of the GDA's existence. If we find out you have talked or you refuse the tasks given to you, we will be forced to terminate you."

They all exchanged glances at each other. "So how much time do we have to decide?" Toshi asked. Jiryen looked at his watch.

"Hmm, none. The Grandmaster has already agreed for you to do it but because I am a nice guy, I will give you all a minute to talk amongst yourselves." As Jiryen, left they all turned to the Grandmaster.

"Father, what is the meaning of this?" Takeda asked, disgruntled and frustrated that they were not consulted.

"I did what was best Takeda. This demon outbreak, it is on a global scale. The original plan was to send you out to hunt them down. But this way you will have proper funding and will be taken care of." Takeda understood, he was still upset.

"But then why not consult us first?" he continued.

"Jiryen appeared in the early hours of the morning; we have been discussing it all night. It was a last minute deal. Please understand. There is no one else I would trust with this other than yourselves." Everyone, although they didn't like being kept out of the loop, knew the Grandmaster was right, it was the best decision.

"Okay, we will do as you request," Takeda responded, everyone nodding in agreement. Jiryen poked his head round the corner.

"Everything good? Good, we need to leave, we have your first mission."

They all stood up. "Already?" Toshi said in disbelief.

"Yes, we need to head to the airport," Jiryen responded. "Go and pack what you need and say your goodbyes. I will meet you outside the main gate." They all nodded. It was all happening so fast, it felt so rushed. They all returned to their bunks to pack up their clothes.

"So, what do we think about this?" Kukiro asked, now that they were alone.

"I think it is a good idea, we need to do something about the demons," Takeda said. Kukiro stopped and turned to him.

"You know what I mean, the GDA? Jiryen?" she asked.

Takeda stopped packing. "I don't know what to think at this point. I say we give them the benefit of the doubt but we watch our backs."

"I agree," Triss jumped in. "I've seen it in the movies; shady government organisations cannot be trusted!" Toshi laughed.

"This isn't a movie Triss. I am sure they are trustworthy but I do agree we need to keep our guard up around them for the moment." Zeke chimed in.

"They seem okay to me, I am just looking forward to fighting some demons!" They all had a little laugh.

The team had just finished packing and left their bunks. They were greeted by a crowd of people, headed by the Grandmaster. In unison, they all bowed to them in respect of the mission they were to undertake. As they all rose, the Grandmaster spoke.

"Although you leave us, you will always have a home here with the Fallen Lotus. Be safe, may you strike fast and first." He hugged Kukiro and Takeda. "Be safe, look out for each other," he whispered in their ears.

"We will," Kukiro responded.

"We won't fail you," Takeda added. They broke apart, smiling, trying hard to hold back the tears of saying goodbye. As they headed to the main gate to begin their mission, Takeda stopped at the statue of Jak. He looked up at her and placed his hand on her statue. He began to whisper to himself, "Goodbye Jak, I will see you soon." He took out from his backpack the dagger that Jak had recovered a long time ago, with the scroll and placed it at the base of the statue. Wiping away a tear, he turned and joined the others.

And that was it, the heroes that defeated Akuma set off to save the world from the hell he had unleashed. Not knowing where their missions would take them, what horrors they would see and what troubles they would encounter. All they knew was that they were together and that no matter what, they wouldn't ever be apart.